THE QUEEN OF DIAMONDS

Leslie Adams doesn't often get angry, upset, or worried. So when Molly, his sister, first disappeared, Les kept calm and used his head. When he was nearly killed in a house explosion while searching for his sister, well, that rattled him a bit, but still Les kept his wits about him.

Now the police are blaming him for the explosion, as well as a botched robbery in which a woman was killed. His schizophrenia is becoming a problem, he's being stalked by a mysterious woman that may or may not exist, and his siblings are questioning his sanity. Understandably, Les is feeling a bit stressed, but he has everything under control. More than that, his delusions are the key to discovering the truth about the robbery and his sister's disappearance. At least, that's what he hopes. The crime debut of a startling new writer!

Borgo Press Books by TRACEY LANDAU

The Queen of Diamonds: A Psychological Mystery

THE QUEEN OF DIAMONDS

A PSYCHOLOGICAL MYSTERY

TRACEY LANDAU

THE BORGO PRESS

MMXIII

THE QUEEN OF DIAMONDS

DEDICATION

For My Little Sister

THE QUEEN OF DIAMONDS

"What happens next?"

"There's…a fire."

"Tell me about the fire."

FLASHES. Explosions. The sounds of thunder, a high-pitched squeal. The air pops. Everything's moving so fast—then it all stops, pauses, and I can clearly see myself. The gun is in my hand. Jimmy is looking at me, but my eyes are glued to the building now engulfed in flames. A frozen image. Had someone seen only that single image—which they had—they'd think I must have done something wrong. That assumption is what got me here.

Jimmy wasn't with me now…figures. Jimmy's always been able to squeeze out of tight situations, using his age as an excuse. Ridiculous. Jimmy's seen more than I will in a lifetime. Sixteen isn't young when you've grown up under the conditions he has. But I'm straying from the story. This isn't about Jimmy—it's about me, as the police continuously remind me. I don't blame them for suspecting me—who seems more threatening? A sixteen-year-old boy that likes to wear his hat backwards, or the twenty-five-year-old guy standing next to him with a gun in one hand and a playing card in the other?

Exactly.

"Tell me about the fire," she repeats herself. The voice is light and unthreatening. It belongs to a psychologist working with my lawyer, working on my case. They're saying I should plead insanity, but that comes later in the story. Or, actually, earlier.

ZOOM.

Things rewind in my mind. I'm outside, now I'm inside. It goes back and forth, first person to third. I'm watching myself. I am myself. SLOW DOWN. The events come to a halt. Another still image. What I see I describe out loud.

"I'm in a bedroom…her bedroom…."

"Go on."

"She's not there."

"Who is 'she'?"

"The non-existing woman."

I call her non-existing because until only recently that's all she's ever been to me. Then again, before I found out she was non-existing, I was very sure she was real, just had no name. I'm not so sure what I believe now.

"She told me to go there."

"A non-existing woman told you to go to a house that, you say, exploded by itself…."

Well, it sounds crazy when she says it like that. I'm about to respond but the movie in my head starts up again. Flip, flip, flip, flash, flash, flash. I hear the reel of film whirl to life. I move farther back in the story, but this time I don't travel so far when someone presses "play".

I'm walking into her bedroom. I see what she wanted me to see—the pictures, a huge slew of photos, scattered all over the floor and the bed. The bed…it's neatly made. A pink bedcover with black kittens on it. The fan on the desk is on—the culprit for the mess; the papers and photos fly all over the room like they're alive. Jimmy turns the fan off. We're silent as we look around the room. Was the gun in my hand or his? I can't remember—it flashes back and forth between us like a ghost in our hands. I walk around looking for something, but I'm not sure what. Maybe an explanation. Maybe I'm waiting for a whole bunch of people to just jump out and say "Surprise!" as if it was all one big practical joke, so it could all be over. Like hell it would.

"There are pictures everywhere," I hear myself telling the psychologist.

"What's in the pictures?"

There's a moment.

"Me," I say.

ZOOM! I'm off again. Jimmy hears something and goes running into the hall with the gun. I'm looking all over the place, checking under the bed, which upsets the cat which scratches my face...shit...that cat must've died in the explosion.

Okay, stop thinking about the cat.

"Poor cat," I hear myself say. The delayed transfer of thoughts into words annoys me, but then that doesn't matter when I see her...or it, rather. The playing card. The Queen of Diamonds.

Things slow to a steady pace, live time. I pick up the card. I hear Jimmy scream.

"Get out of here, let's get out of here! She isn't here,

it's a trap. Come on, let's go!"

Jimmy grabs my arm and pulls me from the room. Now I'm back outside again, the house ablaze before me.

"You told me earlier you found something in the house. What did you find?"

"A playing card. The Queen of Diamonds." I don't even hesitate.

"So let me understand something.... Were you there to rob the house?" I hear her ask. I feel myself shake my head. The film in my head hasn't stopped. I watch as Jimmy and I head down the street, only to meet a half dozen cop cars. Fast forward. I'm walking into the police station. Jimmy's sister is already waiting there to pick him up. Then I think of my sister.

My sister is the youngest of my parents' offspring. I'm the oldest. Two brothers divide us. The reason I think about my sister is because she's the reason this whole, crazy journey began.

"My sister...," I mumble.

"Is that who you were looking for?"

"Yes...." *No....*

"No...." *Yes...?*

"Maybe...." I don't have time to answer that question, things are moving again. Now it's going backwards...far, far back, back to the very beginning. All the images of what happened between then and now move so quickly my head starts to pound. I'm groaning, grabbing at my head, pulling my hair.

"Stop...," I whisper to the darting images, but they're

out of my control.

"Stop!" I yell louder. Nothing's changing. I feel like my head's going to explode when I hear the woman's voice again.

"I'm going to count backwards from ten. When I reach one and snap my fingers, you will wake up feeling refreshed. 10...9...8...7...."

I want her to hurry up. I feel myself sliding away from the memories, but my head's still throbbing and I'm starting to scream.

"...5...4...3...2...*1*!"

SNAP.

I'm awake. I look into the woman's face and realize I've completely forgotten what I told her or what I was just thinking about. I hope it didn't sound crazy. By the looks of it, however, I don't seem so fortunate.

The psychologist is hurried out of the room by my lawyer and I'm alone—other than a policeman who stands in the corner, staring at me, but not in the mood to talk. I stare at my reflection in the two-way. "*Blue*," I think. I know there's someone on the other side of that glass.... Positive of it. I only hope I'm staring whoever it is right in the face, wishing to convey through my stare my innocence. Like hell it would. I don't even know if I'm innocent—though I deeply hope that I am.

The person staring back at me in the mirror is twenty-five. His name is Leslie Gregory Adams, and he's a soon-to-be-medicated schizophrenic. Perhaps I should explain....

I have wacky parents, hence the embarrassing name.

I go by Les. I'm a professional dancer working in NYC—and no, I'm not gay. I have a girlfriend. Her name is Jenny. She's funny, artsy,and scares me with her neverending supply of energy. I have a dog. His name is Bongo. He too scares me with his never-ending supply of energy, but he's a puppy. Hopefully, his heart is strong enough to take it.

But I suppose none of that matters after the "I'm a schizophrenic" thing. The psychologist who evaluated me when I was younger believed that my condition existed because I don't act on my emotions, but instead keep them bottled up. I must agree. I never get mad. I never get upset, sad, or worried. I'm almost always happy. Apparently that's a bad thing.

Other than having a very, *very* realistic imaginary friend when I was younger, my condition was so mild my parents feared that medication would only worsen my illness. Until now I've been able to handle things just fine by maintaining a healthy diet and, most importantly, exercising regularly.

Several weeks ago I came back to Jersey to visit my family and heal from a sprained ankle. What was meant to be a weekend visit ended up being a month-long stay. This entire time I haven't been able to properly exercise, and now I'm here. I've undoubtedly been seeing things, but something else, something bigger than that has been unfolding these past few weeks. Something Jimmy and I, and now the police, are trying to figure out.

When the lawyer and psychologist come back into

the room, they bring with them someone I wasn't expecting.

"Danny?" My gay brother.

"Les!" He runs over to me and sits in the chair facing mine. The reflection of myself is blocked, along with my connection with whoever was on the other side of that mirror.

"Danny, where is everyone? Where's Mom and Dad?"

"They went out to eat, they don't know—listen, I got your message, what the hell—"

"What about Mark? Where's Mark?" My other brother.

"He's fine! He's going to check up on Jimmy, figure out what's going on; now what the *hell* happened?"

"I went to her house, Danny. She had pictures of me all over the place—I'm guessing she stole them from Molly's house, or our parents. Listen, she knew I was coming; I was looking around when Jimmy grabbed me and got us out of there right before the place exploded—"

"Les…this woman isn't *real*!"

I pull the card out of my jacket pocket. Until now I was able to keep it from the police, but holding onto it didn't matter anymore. As long as someone other than me, someone I could trust, saw the card, it will have fulfilled its purpose. I throw the card onto the table. It lands with a slap, the little rectangle laying there perfectly centered on the table. I could see the expression change on Danny's face.

"Is that real?" I ask him. He nods silently, then his eyes light up and I could tell he's running all sorts of thoughts and explanations through his mind. At least he believes me now.

"Les, how the hell am I supposed to get you out of here? Out of this whole thing? It's not like I can just bail you out or something, you're under investigation! They think you're crazy, what am I supposed to do— what do you want me to do?!"

I can't answer that. I have to admit, it's an excellent question.

"Okay, okay," Danny is out of his seat now. I could tell he's going to do a better job at figuring things out than I could. I should be listening to him, but something else in the room catches my attention. There's someone looking at me in the mirror that hadn't been there a second ago. I turn around, expecting to see the redheaded kid in the hoodie behind me. There are a few people there; my lawyer, the psychologist, the cop, but no redhead. I look back at the mirror. The kid is mouthing something to me; I just can't make out what it is.

"Danny...," I whisper. Danny isn't listening to me. He's busy being a lawyer about the situation, going over my rights and yelling at the policeman, saying it isn't legal to keep me here without any substantial evidence, blah blah....

I could hear him. I could hear the boy whispering something to me; I have to make out the words. I realize this is a figment; a non-existing person created by my panicked, nervous little mind, so I close my eyes and concentrate. What am I trying to tell myself?

It was a sunny afternoon when I left for my sister's house. She lived only a town over from our parents. I never understood that about my family; everyone but me has lived in the same area all their lives.

Molly, my sister, was not at the station. She said she would be. It wasn't too much of a problem. When I called her phone and she didn't pick up, I figured she was at work or something. Like I mentioned earlier, I don't often get worried. I called my parents. They picked me up and brought me to their house, promising to keep me just for lunch....

RED. I open my eyes but the figment's gone. He was a redhead, wearing red, whispering red...what the hell did "red" mean? Was I trying to remind myself of something? It would've helped if the message was a little more descriptive than "red."

"What do you mean he was armed with an 'unregistered weapon'?" I hear my brother shout. I cringe. I should've mentioned that to him.

The simple way of explaining the gun is to say that it's Jimmy's. Jimmy is sixteen and should not have a gun, so obviously he doesn't have it registered. How he got the gun is another ordeal that isn't important right now. None of that is too important anymore because the policeman has just grabbed my brother and is now pulling him from the room. The last thing I need is for Danny to get arrested too and have my parents find out what's going on. That would ruin everything. Then they'd tell the police and we'd never find Molly....

Okay, so Molly is missing. She has been missing for quite some time, but how long exactly is unclear, as is everything else in this mess. My brothers Danny and Mark know about this. My parents do not. The reason we have decided not to tell our parents about her disappearance is because the situation is all very delicate. We still aren't sure whether or not Molly disappeared intentionally. If it was intentional, then it's much more important *not* to find her. I'll get back to that whole thing later.

"Danny, it's okay, I'll talk to you later. Just go meet up with Mark, find out if there's any new information. Can you do that for me?"

Danny is unsatisfied by my response, protesting, "Yeah, then what about you?"

"He's being transferred to a holding cell at the Manchasen Hospital for the Criminally Insane," the cop growls.

"WHAT?" My brother shouts.

"WHAT?" I echo him.

But the cop has disappeared through the door with my brother. Danny's fingertips clawing at the doorframe is the last I see of him before the psychologist places herself in front of me.

"Leslie," she says softly. She tries to hold my hand but I won't let her touch me. I should be going nuts right now, having just been told I'm going to be locked up, but I'm not. In fact, the only thing that worries me is that I'm not worried.

"Les, we'll be meeting with the judge tomorrow to discuss where you'll be held until your court date, as well as when your court date is," my lawyer says very matter-of-factly. She's much rougher and edgier than the psychologist. Had the two of them been officers, she'd be the bad cop. It's not a bad thing. There's power in her voice; I'm sure that if I can convince her I'm innocent, she could easily convince a jury.

The cop's back in the room with a couple of detectives, guys that look like they just walked out of *Law and Order*. My public defender's expression turns darkly serious when she sees them. I can't help but notice the situation has turned into a battle of the sexes.

"Could we have a moment?" one of the men was going to ask, but my lawyer jumps the question on "could".

"You've had your chance, and my client's undoubtedly exhausted. Are you aware that it's 3:20 a.m.?"

How time flies.

The cop pulls me from my chair rather roughly—by now I've come to the conclusion that for whatever reason, he just doesn't like me. He cuffs my hands behind my back. I guess I'll be taken to the institution in a police car. As I'm being escorted out of the room I stare the two men in the eyes, trying to read their minds. *BLUE....* They were the ones behind the mirror.

A little about me: I have a gift. I credit my mild schizophrenia for my gift. Ever since I was a boy I've been able to guess what people are thinking. It's not nearly as interesting as it sounds. I can only read colors, cards, and numbers. Think of a number, 1-1,000: I'll guess it. Think of a color, anything you want: I'll name the color on the first try. Think of a card, I'll read your mind. I'm hardly ever wrong. The cheap trick is good for picking up girls and winning bets, but little else. The most useful thing about the talent, however, is it helps me remember who people are. Miranda has seven hearts, eighty-five is Kelly's lucky number, Charlie likes green. That sort of thing. These detectives, both of them…they were blue. *Who was red?*

"So, have you banged your new girlfriend yet?" was the first thing my father said to me after my parents picked me up at the train station. I was instantly relieved that Jenny hadn't joined me on this trip.

"Marty, don't be so nosey…! Of course he has," my mother responded. She waited until my father got in the car to whisper "Always use protection," into my ear.

In the car they asked me how Jenny and Bongo were doing. I told them Bongo hadn't had a heart attack yet. They were pleasantly shocked. I told them they should visit me in New York.

My mother: "Oh, yes, certainly!"

My father: "We'd never find a parking space."

"You could take the train," I suggested.

"I mean at the train station! Did you see how packed that lot was? Anywho, if we have to drive all the way to the train station, we might as well drive the whole way to New York! Ah, here we are; home sweet home!"

We were already at the house. There was no use in pointing out the house is only a block away from the train station; my dad refuses to walk anywhere. And yet they still keep his treadmill in the basement. As we sat down to eat, my mom gave me the update on all my siblings.

"Mark's got a new dangerous hobby. He's picked up drag racing—thinks we don't know. I don't get it, he doesn't even like cars; he works at a pet store, for Pete's sake! You have to talk him out of it, or else that boy's going to get himself killed. Oh, by the way, you should ask him for some dog food while you're here; he can get it for you at a discount, you know. Molly's started medical school, looks like she's going to stick with it— probably why she wasn't there to pick you up. She's got this lovely new roommate, a girl named Triste? Trish, is that it? Some sort of bizarre name—Oh!" She stopped and smiled at me. "Danny has a boyfriend!"

"Oh really?"

"Mmm-hmm. His name is Derek."

"You meet him yet?"

"Well, no, but he sounds sweet.... He's into theatre. You two should meet each other."

"Mmm-hmm."

"Oh, and...." She put down her fork and looked at me sorrowfully. "I have some sad news. Do remember Dr. Patricia?"

"You mean my psychologist?"

"No, no, not Dr. Massy. Dr. Patricia was the child

therapist? You had a few sessions at her house when Dr. Massy was gone on her honeymoon."

"Oh, right! She had that cool house? Nice house...."

"She was killed about a week ago. Someone was robbing the house; the police think she got in the way."

"What? That's crazy!"

"Yeah, she was a sweet woman," my father said getting up. "Now, how about I drive you to Molly's? She's probably remembered that she forgot you by now. Might as well get you there, before she starts worrying."

The police car comes to a sudden stop and I smash into the seat in front of me. It looks like we've already reached the hospital. Did I sleep? I must have, it's 4:18. No wonder the cop's in a bad mood.

The cop pulls me out of the car and before me stands that creepy, rotting old building that's in all those scary movies. The huge building towers over me, cold and intimidating. I'm waiting to see a flash of lightning and hear rolling thunder. As the cop forces me up the steps, I can tell I must be afraid because all around me I'm hearing voices whispering...voices belonging to no one.

"Voices of the dead, voices of the insane," one says by my ear. I've decided I hate this place.

"Apartment 208. There should be a spare key hidden in the potted plant," my father told me when I got out of the car. I bid him farewell and headed up for Molly's apartment.

I dug through that potted plant for what must've been ten minutes, only to find the key was hidden *under* it, not *in* it. I picked up the key and put it in the lock when someone shouted, "Who the hell are you?"

I turned around and came face to face with a tall girl with blinding blonde hair.

"What? Hi! Um, I'm Les?"

"All right, Les, what the hell are you doing with that key?"

I look at the key, then back at the girl.

"What? Oh! Oh, are you Trish?"

"Trish…yes, who are you?"

"I'm Molly's brother."

"Molly's broth—Oh! Right! Sorry, here, come in!" She unlocked the door and went inside. "By the way, have you seen Molly? I've been looking for her."

"No, actually. She was supposed to pick me up at the train station but she didn't show.…"

FREEZE. Wait a minute.… Rewind. I found the key under the potted plant. Was that when I first met Trish? Or was it later?

BUZZ. The cell door clatters as it opens, the metal grinding as the bars wheel back and my room is presented to me. Well, at least it isn't white and pillowy.

I might as well be in jail—there is a cot in one corner, a toilet in the other, and above a barred window. There are carvings all over the walls, even messages written in blood…I wonder if they are really there.…

The cop throws me on the cot, then realizes he forgot to un-cuff me. After he takes the cuffs off and leaves the room, a cute young nurse takes his place. She'd seem sweet if she wasn't pushing pills in my face.

"There you go, drink them down with water—"

"What are these?"

"They're pills to help you sleep. Go ahead, drink them down—"

"What *are* these?" I demand. "I've never taken medication before, for mental illness *or* sleep. How do you know I won't react to this stuff?"

"A reaction is what we want, now take them."

"Well, that sounds grave."

Two guys come out of nowhere and push me flat against the wall. Even the nurse is unexpectedly strong. She forces the pills right down my throat, which I much prefer over the needle one of the orderlies has with him. I choke trying to swallow the meds, grab the water from the nurse and drink it down, but still there's a lump in my throat. The nurse smiles at me. I don't smile back.

The orderlies let go of me, the nurse steps aside and again I see the redhead. He's whispering to me again, but his figure is flickering like static. I frown. The whole room is going in and out of focus. Whatever they gave me, it's doing its job.

I'm out before the nurse gets back to her office.

I'm walking around in Molly's apartment. She's fighting with someone on the phone. I stand there awkwardly, trying to decide whether or not I should enter. The walls breathe—the whole apartment expands and then starts to compress. I'm being squeezed against the floor and the ceiling.

Lightning. The phone rings. I pick it up.

"Hello?" No one answers. Gasoline drips out of the receiver. The entire thing melts and slips between my fingers, like I'm in a Dalí painting.

"Hello!"

The voice comes from behind me. I turn around and Scott is standing there smiling.

"You're not—" I start.

"Lying," he interrupts. He hands me a playing card with an empty front. Then, in the center of the white, a number appears. Twenty-two. Scott shakes his head.

"Les?"

The bubble bursts. I open my eyes then quickly shut them, the light too much for me to handle. *Where am I?*

"He's still drowsy from the medication."

"Where…," I try to say, but my throat is sour. I attempt to open my eyes again. For a quick moment I see a flash of something or someone. I can't think straight—god, I *hate* meds.

"Les?"

"Who *is* that?!" I shout. The voices are scrambled. Now a bunch of people are speaking very, very quickly. I keep my head in my hands the entire time, but I can sense that I'm being moved. I'm sitting, I'm standing, I'm sitting again. When will these drugs wear off?

…Desk.

I'm staring at a desk. It's a clear, glass desk with papers and pens and little else. How long have I been staring at this table? I blink a little and look around.

I'm in an office. It has a wood and dark green color scheme, making the desk seem a little out of place. There are wood bookshelves with books and busts. I look down and see I'm sitting on a wooden chair...a nice one. I realize it's padded and surprisingly comfortable...*I like this chair.* I'm wearing the same shoes I was wearing the night before (probably all the same clothes as last night) and below my shoes I see my reflection in the nicely polished wood floor. Wait... *does this chair have wheels?*

I squeak around in the chair a little. It glides gently across the floor.

It *does* have wheels! *This chair has it all!* I'm smiling at the floor, then suddenly have the strong feeling that I'm being watched. I look next to me. My lawyer is sitting there, her fingers tightly knitted together on her lap. She's well dressed and staring at me. I hear a creak and look forward. On the other side of the desk sits a big black man in a Judge's robe.... Oh, dear god....

"*Where am I?*" I whisper rather obviously to my lawyer. She seems shocked with the question. The awkward silence hangs in the air as thick as marmalade. Then the man bursts out laughing.

He laughs for what must be ten minutes, a hoarse, deep laugh that goes up and down in pitch. I don't blame him, really. I'd probably laugh at me too. I sit watching him, patient and rather bewildered, a sheepish smile plastered across my face. My lawyer is just as pleasantly confused as I am.

With some difficulty he finally catches his breath and looks at me. He opens his mouth to say something, then bursts out laughing again.

Molly didn't come home at all that night. Trish didn't prove to be much company either.

"So, when did you and Molly first meet?" I asked. No response.

"You go to the same school as Molly?"

Nothing.

"So…is school hard?"

Silence. The entire time she's looking for something. She's throwing all sorts of things around, flattening herself on the floor to check under the bed, surfing into the labyrinth women call a closet. When I ask her if I could help and what she's looking for, she just waves me away, saying, "No, no, I've got it. Thanks, but I've got it."

Then Trish left.

"You're in your brother Daniel's custody now. Daniel's already accepted you as his responsibility. You must be with him at all times, wherever you go, which means you'll also be staying with him at his place until your court date. Think of it as being under house arrest."

"Minus the house."

"…Even when you are with your brother, you must stay in Sussex County. So no trips, no leaving the state.

You'll be wearing this tracking bracelet until your court date; if something happens like another fire, for example, the police will be able to track everywhere you've been. Don't bother trying to get it off; even if you try to break it, it'll automatically send a signal straight to the police, giving them your exact location."

"Good to know."

"You will also have to attend sessions with Dr. Bandos twice a week until your court date. Do not miss these appointments."

"Got it."

"Lastly,"

When will this end?

"Lastly, you've been ordered to take medication for your schizophrenia—"

"What?" I yell. I stare angrily at my lawyer who doesn't seem surprised by my outburst.

I'm lying back in a blue examination chair, getting the tracking bracelet—this bulky, metallic, indestructible thing—attached to my ankle. If it were my choice, I'd have it put around my wrist, but apparently the police were intent on making the whole experience as uncomfortable as possible. In that regard, they were successful.

"I don't take medication—"

"This is non-negotiable. You're lucky to even get this much; I didn't expect for the judge to go so easy on a schizophrenic—"

"Who's *innocent*," I interject.

"That's for the jury to decide."

What she says stops my train of thought.

"You don't believe I'm innocent?"

"I didn't say that."

That answer isn't good enough for me. She recognizes my discontent.

"I don't think you intended to do anything wrong. I disagree with the prosecution; I don't think you were planning to kill anyone," she adds too quickly.

"But you think I'm the one who blew up the house?"

She takes a breath and shrugs.

"I'm not taking medication."

"Les—"

"Think of a color."

"What?"

Orange. I'll remember that.

Molly woke me up the next morning. I remember our morning together so clearly because it was the first time Molly's ever woken up before me in her life. We ate breakfast at a little diner near her apartment. There she told me everything and more about what school was like and how great it was to live on her own with a fun roommate.

"I met Trish," I said while she was sipping her cup of coffee. She choked and spit it out like a spray all over my face.

"Sorry! Sorry.... Too hot.... When did you meet Trish?"

"Last night," I answered, wiping my face off with a napkin, a little confused. "She was looking for you."

Molly was looking very intense.

"Why? Did she want to tell me something, or.... What? What did she want?"

"I don't know; she was looking around for something. I'm guessing she wanted to ask you if you've seen whatever it was, she didn't tell me."

"Hmm. Well, that makes sense, I guess. She's staying with her mother right now...still moving things into the apartment."

"She did leave—"

"Yeah, she was probably looking for a key or something...."

The conversation died out. Then, abruptly,

"Did you meet Derek? Danny's new boyfriend?"

"No, actually, I haven't even seen Danny yet."

"Oh. Well, Trish is Derek's friend. I met her through Derek, actually—she needed someplace to live for a while. Danny told Derek I had a free room in the apartment, *voilà*. You really should meet him; he's eager to talk with you about New York City and theatre...."

Danny was waiting for me just outside the room. He burst out laughing when he caught sight of the bracelet.

"Because after all, you are just *so* dangerous!" he says pointing to it.

"Well, I think it looks stylish," I joke. My lawyer walks up behind me and puts a hand on my shoulder.

"Your first appointment with Dr. Bandos is tomorrow at noon. This is her card; it has the address on it. Danny doesn't need to stay; he can drop you off and pick you up afterward. Other than that, though, don't go anywhere without him."

"Yes, okay, I've got it—"

"And Les," She leans close to my ear and her voice is soft when she says "Take your medication."

Danny and I watch her leave in silence. She even walks with authority. When she exits, she holds the door open for someone.

"Oh shit," I think out loud as my parents walk through the door. I grab Danny and surprise myself with my frustration.

"You *told* them?!"

"What? No, no, I didn't, I swear!"

"I'm sorry!" I hear and turn to see my brother Mark running in, panting to keep up with my parents. My mother closes the gap between us at an alarming speed.

"WHAT HAPPENED?!" She demands of me. Danny and I look at each other, unsure where to begin. I look past my mother to shout, "I *hate* you!" at Mark.

"Leslie, you come with me this minute!"

"Actually, I have to go with Danny—"

"Danny can drive by himself. Get in the car."

"Well, legally, I *have* to go with Danny…. I'm under his custody."

"*What?*"

Danny points to my ankle. My mother sees the bracelet and squeals.

"Oh my…. What…? What did you…?"

"Oh hey…nice bracelet," my father says, having just caught up with my mother.

"What's going on, are you okay?"

"They locked him up in a mental institution last night, Mom," Mark sneaks in. I can't tell if he's trying to help me or destroy me. My mother gasps. Her eyes turn as big as saucers and she grabs me in a deadly, suffocating hug.

"I miss you," Jenny said on the other side of the phone which seemed just too far away.

"I miss you, too," I tell her back. "I'm actually pretty lonely here."

"I wish I was there!" she moans. "I love your sister."

"Yeah, well you're not missing out. She has so many classes, I hardly ever see her. She says hi, by the way."

"Hi!"

"Jenny, she can't hear you."

"Well, give her the phone."

"She's not here...hence, 'I hardly ever see her'. I'll tell her—ah, beep, did you hear a beep?"

"No."

"It must be another call on this phone, then. Uh...I'll call you later?"

"Sure. Let me know if anything interesting happens. If not, make something up."

"Can do. Bye, love you."

"Love you."

I press buttons on the phone to try and receive the other call. Eventually I hit the right one.

"Hello?" I shout into the empty line. There's a moment before I hear a voice.

"Hello, I'm calling to update you on your travel plans. Your scheduled flight to Hawaii was overbooked, so we'd like to move you to—"

"Wait, I'm sorry," I interrupt the valley girl voice. "I think you mean to be talking to someone else, maybe my sister's roommate. Who are you looking for?"

"Oh, sorry. Who is this?"

"My name's Leslie Adams. My sister lives here with her roommate. Who did you want to speak to?"

"Sir, could I…credit card…name, Molly Adams… moved to…be in?" the line starts to break up. I ask for the woman to repeat the question but the line goes dead.

"What happened?"

"Would you like the cliff notes version, or the long version?"

My parents don't look amused. Mark and Danny sit on either side of me. They look at me and I feel like we're kids again. Since I'm the oldest and calmest, it's always been up to me to get us out of trouble.

"I haven't exercised in a while, I saw some things that weren't there, and I happened to end up at a house that just happened to explode."

"Just happened to…*what*? Are you…? You expect us to believe that?" my mother growls.

"It's true, you can ask Jimmy!"

"Who's Jimmy?"

"This kid—"

"I was told you had a gun on you? Why, and where the hell did you get a gun?"

"It wasn't like I went out and bought a gun; it was Jimmy's."

"Jimmy who? Who is Jimmy?! This 'Jimmy,' is he real?"

Well, that was a good question. For a while I was very unsure of that myself. Jimmy didn't seem real. His exciting stories were unreal, and the way he'd appear where and when you least expected didn't make sense. He also knew things. He knew how to hotwire a car and pick locks. He also seemed to know every aspect of a person's life after only one meeting. More importantly, he knew what I was thinking most of the time—that itself was enough to convince me he was imaginary. It turns out he just happens to make incredible guesses. I decided he must be real when I discovered he couldn't care less if I thought he was imaginary or not. I'll get back to that shortly.

We somehow managed to escape our parents by claiming Danny had to go to work and wherever Danny goes, I must follow.

"Why did you tell them?" I shout at Mark once we decide our parents aren't tailing Danny's car.

"Hey, chill! I needed to see you, and I needed a ride—"

"Use your car!"

"He can't," Danny speaks up. "He crashed it drag racing—"

"And believe me, I didn't want to tell Mom and Dad that either—ooh! Dairy Queen!"

We pass it.

"Damn it!"

"Why did you have to see me? You could've just

called...."

"Well, actually, your number's on my cell, and I lost my cell recently. I haven't had the chance to get to the Verizon store, yet, which reminds me, what kinda phone do you have—"

"The point, Mark, skip to the point."

"Oh, okay, uh.... It has to do with Jimmy, he told me to tell you something...."

"Yes?"

"Uh, you had to meet him somewhere. I think it was today...."

"*Yes?*"

"Damn it."

"You forgot?!"

"Of course," Danny sighs.

"Hey, where are we heading?" Mark asks, pulling at my seat.

"To Jimmy's, where do you think?"

"No, don't!" Mark shouts in my ears. He snaps his fingers, trying to remember. "That was part of his message. He said he has 'friends' hanging around his place, bugging him about why he was at the police station—"

"Gang members just aren't trusting friends, are they?"

"He says not to go looking for him there," Mark finishes, ignoring Danny.

"Then where do we go?" I ask quietly, thinking.

"Well, I have to get to the pet store," Mark groans. "You can drop me off, but Les...."

I turn around and see that Mark is suddenly very serious—a rare occasion with Mark.

"I think you should take the medication. We need to clear this up, and we're never going to find Molly if Danny and I are busy pointing out to you what's real and what's not."

Danny's nodding in agreement.

"I'll think about it," I lie. There's no point in arguing with them now. Right now, we just need to find Jimmy.

"So what do you think?" my sister was shouting at me.

"What?" I could hardly hear her over the music.

"Do you miss going to these kinds of crazy college parties?"

"And being single? No way!"

Molly laughed.

"I'll tell you one thing, I haven't really had a chance to go to any parties this year, what with classes and everything. You're my excuse for being here right now."

"Glad I could help!"

College students were packed everywhere there was a surface. Molly and I sat squished tight on a couch in front of a table stacked with drinks.

"Hey, you should get out there and bust some moves," Molly shouted.

"Somehow I don't think modern dance would work with this crowd."

She laughed again, then challenged me with, "What number am I thinking of?"

"Hmm…208?"

"Ah, but why did I think of that number?"

"Isn't that your apartment number?"

"You're a freak, you know that?"

"Cool trick," Molly and I heard before some kid with a backwards cap and gray hoodie dropped down between us, forcing Molly off the couch. She gave me a look before being eaten up into the crowd, calling "I guess I'll catch up to you?" behind her.

"So, what color am I thinking of?" the boy asked, engrossed.

"Red."

"Awesome. That helps get chicks, doesn't it?"

"That was my sister."

"Ahh.…" The boy looked back at the spot where Molly had disappeared. "So…she single?"

"Here, you want me to guess something else for you?"

"Sure!" The kid turned to face me again.

"All right, think of your age."

"Okay. Wait—"

"Sixteen."

"Hey!"

"Little young to be at a party like this, aren't you?"

"You know, you really should charge for this stuff." He gave me a funny look, his eyebrows rising and lowering along with this ridiculous smile and I couldn't help but laugh.

It was the first time I met Jimmy. I never expected to so much as catch a glimpse of him again…now I can't imagine being in New Jersey and not seeing him somewhere bizarre.

Danny and I arrive at the theatre maybe fifteen minutes after dropping Mark off. The curtains are pulled back, revealing a set that seems to be coming together quite nicely. The play being performed is *Man with Bags* and the stage looks twisted and bizarre. Being a surrealism fanatic, I'm eager to see the end product.

We decided in the car to meet up with Derek. Derek's an actor and Danny's prop master—has been for every production in the last four years. It was through this production that Danny and Derek met, although apparently Derek's lived in the town over from us for years.

I pay close attention now to who's sitting around reading their lines in the auditorium seats. Unfortunately I don't see her there, the mysterious unknown woman. Instead I catch sight of Brendan—a member of the cast I met recently.

"Hey, Danny, I'll catch up with you later," I call to him before heading towards Brendan.

Brendan's wearing yet another piece of *42nd Street* merchandise (I've come to realize he's an avid fan). This time it's a hat. I sit down in the seat next to him, causing him to look up from his script.

"Oh, hey...Les, right?"

"Yep."

"Are you looking for your brother, or...."

"Actually I'm looking for someone else; a woman with dark brown hair, heavy black makeup, kind of goth?"

"All right, you're describing a third of the cast."

"No, she's not an actor. She's...she's a smoker, always has this strange, secretive smile on her face?"

"Oh, I know who you're talking about. Sorry, I haven't seen her."

Of course. I sigh. "I suppose you don't know her name?"

"Sorry."

I thank him and get up to leave when he pulls me back into my seat.

"You know, we have a rehearsal tonight. She might be here then."

"Yeah? Hey, could you do me a favor? Could you get Derek—you know Derek, right? Could you get him to call me or Danny if she shows up tonight? Please?"

"Sure, no problem.... Okay, is it just me going crazy, or can you hear that too?"

"What?" I say before I realize my cell phone is ringing. I fumble in my pocket, grab it out and see a number I don't recognize. I pick it up and am immediately greeted by Jimmy's voice.

"Get to the Quick Check now, you know the one."

"Wait, wait, wait! Jimmy, what's going on?"

"Get here now."

"Okay, I'll grab Danny and—"

"No, no, no, no! Don't bring your brother, just you."

"But...I can't! I don't know if anyone's told you yet, but they're blaming the fire on me. I got a tracking anklet now, and I'm supposed to stick with Danny or—"

"No. No Danny."

"I *can't*."

"Steal your brother's car, just for an hour, and get over here!"

"Jimmy!"

He hangs up.

I wait for a moment, the phone still at my ear, dumbly expecting him to call back.

"Wait.… What fire? You were arrested?" Brendan asks me, having listened to the entire conversation. I stutter something and leave him sitting there confused and curious.

It was ironic and typical Jimmy that he wanted to meet at the Quick Check. The little store was the last place Jimmy should be hanging around.… That's a long story, I'll get to it later.

I walk up and down the theater aisle, trying to decide what to do. It's in situations like these where schizophrenia sometimes comes in handy.

"Go," I hear.

"He can't go!" Another voice argues.

I'm suddenly put in the very awkward position of hearing my thoughts out loud. I stand still, my head turning back and forth as the two voices debate.

"It's important. Jimmy told you to get there now, so go."

"He can't just leave; he has to grab Danny first. Jimmy doesn't understand how important it is that—"

"Jimmy explicitly told you *not* to bring Danny."

"If he doesn't bring Danny, he's breaking the law."

"Because the cops are magically going to find out Danny's not with him? It's just an hour, and how are the police going to know?"

"It doesn't matter; he doesn't even have the car keys. He might as well go with Danny."

"He has the keys."

"No, he doesn't—"

"They're in his pocket."

What? I fumble in my pockets and am surprised to find that the keys are indeed there. It creeps me out for a moment, then I remember Danny had thrown me his keys, saying he had no pockets and wanted me to hold on to them.

Seeing the key in my hand makes me nervous. I shift my weight impatiently, then, hoping no one will see me, I moan to the voices, "I can't do this, Danny's going to kill me."

"So call him and tell him you're borrowing the car on the way there. Problem solved."

"Okay, that's one option. Voice #2, what do you think?" I ask the air.

"You really shouldn't—"

"Sounds good," I tell myself as I run out of the theatre to Danny's red car. It suddenly reminds of the imaginary redhead from the police station. Now I realize what he was trying to tell me....

Miranda has seven hearts. Eighty-five is Kelly's lucky number. Charlie likes green.

Jimmy's color is red.

"Ooh, you're taking me to see a play?" I asked Molly as we pulled up into the theatre parking lot.

"Nope."

I was disappointed.

"I'm going to introduce you to Derek!"

Less disappointed.

"He's playing one of the lead roles. He really wants to meet you—you two can talk theatre together." She said that last part in a proper British accent.

"What's the play?"

"It's called *Man with Bags*? Some theatre-of-the-absurd piece. Derek read me something from it; it sounds like the main character is walking around in a dream. You'd love it, of course. It's driving Danny crazy because they have, like, fifty different suitcases as props."

When we walked in a rehearsal was in progress on stage. "Take a seat," Molly whispered to me. "I'll go check if Derek's here."

I obeyed and took a seat in the sea of empty chairs. The moment I sat down I heard a whisper from behind me; a quiet voice that slithered through the air and into my ear.

"Ballet?" It asked. I turned around and that's when I saw the non-existing woman for the first time. She wore a scarlet smile of silent amusement on a pale white face that looked bright against her dark attire. It took me a moment to realize she'd spoken to me.

"Excuse me?"

"You're a dancer. Ballet?"

"Modern and contemporary, mostly."

"You're not gay, though."

I smiled, intrigued. "No.… How did you—?"

"You glided to your seat, and before that you glided down the aisle. Dancers have a very distinct way of walking. As for the gay thing, I have excellent gay-dar. It's my bizarre little talent."

"Impressive."

"And you?"

"What about me?"

"What's your bizarre little talent?"

"Hmm.… I guess.… I can read minds."

"Oh?"

"Just colors, numbers, sometimes cards."

"I have a card in mind. Humor me?"

"Queen of…Diamonds."

She smiled wider, showing some sparkling white teeth between her ruby red lips. "What a handy little trick."

"Hardly. Are you in the play?"

She shook her head. "My friend is."

"Well, it's nice to meet you. Your name is…?" I offered my hand, but she rose from her seat, still smiling, and walked away. I watched her leave in awe.

Well she's an interesting character, I thought to myself. It was a moment later that Molly found me again.

"Derek's in the back," she whispered to me before leading me in the opposite direction the non-existing woman had gone.

I find Jimmy in the Quick Check talking to the clerk, an old man with a crooked back and enthusiastic voice.

"Next time those punk-ass kids aren't going to be so lucky," the man was cackling. Jimmy looks coolly amused. He notices me and smiles.

"Les, there you are! Mr. Thompson here was just telling me he was robbed for the third time. He said you were taken hostage?!"

"Damn brats—one pointed a gun right in my face! Can you believe that? So you got away all right?" the clerk asks, wide-eyed, recognizing me.

"Yeah, well, I ran for it when they weren't looking," I lie.

"Mr. Thompson bought a shotgun," Jimmy tells me.

"Can't wait for those shit-for-brains to try that again.… Next time, I'll be ready, don't you worry about that!" the clerk cackles again.

"Isn't he clever?" Jimmy says with a smile.

…Okay, let me explain.

Molly needed groceries. She was far too busy with work and classes to shop, so I offered to help, having nothing better to do. It was night and I didn't have a car, so I chose the closest store to the apartment. That store was the Quick Check.

The store isn't rundown, but it isn't in the best part of town. The shop had been robbed twice in one month, by the same group. I didn't know that. I also didn't know the robbers had planned a third visit.

Imagine this, if you will: You're walking down the aisles of this empty store. It's quiet. You're content, a little tired maybe. You have everything you need in a basket and are ready to check out so you can get back home, lay on a couch, and watch TV with a bag of Cheetos. But the closer you get to the front of the store, the more aware you become that there's some sort of commotion going at the check-out counter. You hear yelling. People are cursing. Now you're finally at the end of the aisle. You peek out, expecting, perhaps, to see the clerk arguing with some difficult customers. You don't expect those customers to be a couple of guys in ski masks pointing a gun in the angry clerk's face.

I was frozen. I blinked, expecting the men to disappear, but they didn't. As the robbers and cashier screamed curses back and forth at each other, a few thoughts popped into my head.

1. That cashier is insane, why doesn't he just hand over the money already?
2. *I'm* insane. Maybe none of this is real....
3. They haven't noticed me yet.

Thought 3 set me in motion. I started looking for exits.

"Come on, just hand over the money!" the robber not holding the gun yelled.

"Go rob some other store, I'm not handing nothing over!" the cashier screamed back.

I quietly put down the basket of junk foods and slowly started walking backwards towards the emergency exit. I kept looking forward, listening to the robbery and hoping no one would check my aisle.

When I decided I must be close to the end of the aisle, I turned around to run, and…SLAM!

A third robber and I fell to the floor. The sound of our collision startled the other two robbers and the cashier.

"What the hell?!" Robber 3 yelled, angrily getting to his feet. He looked at me and dug a swish blade out of his pocket. *Shit*, I thought. Robber 1 with the gun showed up and pointed the revolver at me.

"Stand up, hostage," he said. I calmly obeyed and realized I wasn't as worried as I should be.

"Fine! Here! Take the freakin' money," the cashier growled. He grabbed the cash register drawer, pulled it loose, and threw it down on the checkout counter, causing change to fly everywhere. Robber 2 grabbed as many bills as he could and yelled back to his associates, "Let's get out of here!"

Robber 1 looked at Robber 3, who looked at me, put away the knife, and ran over to help Robber 2 collect more money. Then Robber 1 started staring at me.

"Let the poor guy go, you don't need him!" the cashier barked. He was standing at the front of the aisle, now, his eyes darting nervously back and forth between the robbers taking his money and me. Robber 1 with the gun shouted back, "Don't worry, old man. We're not going to hurt him."

His voice was somehow familiar.

"Come on, let's go! What you waiting for?" Robber 2 said as he ran over to Robber 1. Robber 1 whispered in his ear. Robber 2 and Robber 1 both looked at me and laughed.

Now I was getting nervous.

Robber 3 finally came over, looking annoyed. "Let's go!"

"All right." Robber 1 pushed me in front of him and pressed the gun in my back. "Walk."

Oh shit oh shit oh shit, I thought as the four of us left the store. A crappy little car with no license plate sat waiting half on the curb. Robber 3 jumped behind the steering wheel, Robber 2 sat shotgun, and I was pushed into the smelly backseat next to Robber 1 who kept his gun on me. The three doors closed simultaneously and the car sputtered away from the store, my groceries, and Molly's shopping list.

What the hell am I doing here? I thought to myself as Robber 2 whispered something in Robber 3's ear. He smiled and looked at me in the rear view mirror. The short guy with the gun sitting next to me stared at me the whole car ride. I stared out the window and listened to the car's gasping, clattering sounds as we drove on. We all sat in silence.

Eventually we came to a rotting building complex. The car putted to a slow chug, bumped up onto the curb, and died. The robbers in the front turned around and waited for commands from the short guy with the gun.

"Leave us," he said menacingly. "I'll see you guys later."

They nodded, got out of the car and scattered, disappearing like shadows into the night.

Now I was alone with the guy with the gun and familiar voice. We sat in the car and stared at each other. *SHIT SHIT SHIT*, I thought. There was silence for what must've been only five minutes, but felt like a lifetime, when the guy with the gun finally spoke.

"What number am I thinking of?"

Not what I was expecting.

"Wh-What? Uh…eighty-nine?"

"*Aaawesome.* Like I said, dude, you can make money off of that!"

I sat dumbly staring at him, completely confused. He laughed and pulled off the ski mask, revealing a young, smiling face.

"Remember me? Jimmy? From the party?" he laughed.

I was still confused. He slapped me on the back and kept laughing. He seemed happy enough, so I ventured to ask, "You're not going to shoot me, are me?"

He seemed surprised. "What? No! Of course not! It's not even loaded."

He threw the gun into the front, causing me to flinch.

"Just, you know, don't tell anyone about this…I mean…. You're not gonna say nothing to the cops, right? Cause I can *get* bullets."

"NO, no," I answered quickly. "My lips are sealed."

The boy smiled again. "Good. Hey, chill out dude! Man, you should see your face right now."

"Yeah, okay…you just robbed that guy."

"Yeah, don't worry about it; we do it all the time. See, we only really steal back the amount we've spent there. The three of us, we shop there all the time."

"Um.... What?"

"Yeah! Mr. Thompson, the manager, he's a great guy. Known him for years."

"Okay...."

"The way we see it, this guy runs a convenience store all day. All he does. He isn't a doctor, or a lawyer. He never went to college. Doesn't have any kids, isn't married. He just owns a convenience store." Jimmy smiled. "We add some excitement to his life!"

This kid's twisted, I thought, but I smiled and nodded. He asked me what I was doing there and I told him about Molly's shopping list.

"Ah, the hot sister! Well, listen, Thompson's probably closed up by now. Or he's talking to the police, whatever. Let me buy you a drink to make it up to you."

He scrambled into the front seat and threw the gun into the glove compartment.

"We'll have to use your ID though...left my fake one at home," he said as he twisted the key in the ignition, forcing the car coughing back to life.

I've never been one to turn down a free drink. So, realizing I had nothing better to do, I accepted his invitation. That night Jimmy and I swapped hundreds of stories, drank heavily, and had a surprisingly good time. He told me about his phobias of bees and buttons and most things starting with B, and I told him about my schizophrenia. We exchanged cell phone numbers.

A little while later when I found out Molly was

missing, strangely, he was the first one I told.

"Isn't that crazy, Les? The same robbers, three times," Jimmy smirks at me.

"If they knew what was good for them, they'd stop robbing this place, especially now that he has a *gun*," I say rather pointedly to Jimmy.

He smiles at me sadly. "Yeah, I know what you mean."

"So you'll stop?" I ask him later when we're alone in the back of the store by the drinks.

"Yeah, yeah…I'll find somewhere else to shop," Jimmy grumbles.

"You're ridiculous. So, why'd you call me?"

"I didn't call you."

I freeze. "Wait.… What?"

He looks at me, confused. *Was I imagining his phone call?* I start thinking back when Jimmy cracks up.

"Yeah, nah, I'm just kidding, I called you. Damn, you thought you were going all schizo, didn't ya?"

"Jimmy! What did you want to tell me?"

"Cop."

"What?"

Jimmy grabs me and hides me behind a rack of chips. We're kneeling on the floor and at first I'm not sure why.

"There's a cop over there," Jimmy whispers.

"I thought you said no one knew you were one of the robbers?"

"Not me, you!" He points to the tracking bracelet around my ankle.

"Shit. You don't think…."

"Calm down."

"Shit, shit, shit."

"Calm down!" he hisses at me. "He's probably just here for a doughnut or something."

I peak over the rack and see the cop by the baked goods. I kneel back down and the realization hits me.

"That's the cop from the police station!" I whisper.

"Les, all cops are from police stations,"

"I mean the one who hates me! The one who was there when I was brought in and questioned and put under hypnosis—"

"You were put under hypnosis? That's crazy!"

"He knows I'm a schizophrenic. He's going to see this tracking thing and put two and two together! I should've just brought Danny along."

"All right, I see why you're upset."

"We've got to get out of here before he sees me."

"Try the bathroom; it might have a window," a voice belonging to neither me nor Jimmy says. For a second I think we've been discovered by the cop. Then I turn around and see Scott.

Oh no, I think.

"Listen, I know what you're thinking, but yell at me later. You know you can trust me to get you out of this," Scott tells me.

I know he's right, but I'm afraid to trust him. I look at Jimmy who's looking at me, waiting.

"Jimmy, bathroom."

"What? Go later!"

"No, I mean there might be a way out."

Scott smiles, pleased that I'm listening to him.

We sneak into the bathroom and close the door quietly behind us. I look around the tight room. No windows.

"Great job, Scott," I growl. Scott shrugs and Jimmy looks at me confused.

"I'm Jimmy."

"I know."

"You called me Scott."

"No, I didn't. I called Scott 'Scott'." I ignore Jimmy's puzzled expression and watch Scott circle the room, thinking of a way to get us out. He would come up with something, too—he always did.

Scott was that very, very realistic imaginary friend I had when I was a little kid. I mentioned him earlier. I never forgave him for trying to turn me against my family.... See, when my parents found out Scott wasn't an "imaginary friend" but a schizophrenic manifestation, they tried to convince me he was fake. He retaliated by trying to convince me to run away from home.

Other than aging with me, he's always looked exactly the same: Scott has spiky purple hair, clear, pale skin, and dark, purple eyes. He wears a florescent light green jacket, a black and white striped T-shirt, black pants, and checkered Converse sneakers. It never changes, and despite these peculiarities, he's always seemed so real to me. It's hard to just ignore him and accept he's nothing more than a mirage.

I catch myself believing in him now.

"Scott isn't real," I tell Jimmy and try to ignore Scott's hurt expression. It gets my heart pumping like I just got into a fight with a close friend—which, I suppose, Scott was.

"Les, meet Derek. Derek, this is my brother, Les," Molly introduces us.

I shook Derek's hand and said hi. Derek had one of those familiar faces, dirty blond hair, and introspective brown eyes. I could see Danny's interest in him when Derek's face lit up into a bright smile, looking warm and receptive.

"So Danny tells me you're a real success story! Actor on Broadway, right?"

"I don't know where he's getting that from. No; I'd like to act, but I'm mostly focused on dance."

"Don't downplay it!" Molly interrupted. She beamed at Derek before continuing with "He's a professional dancer who's worked at all the prestigious dance companies in New York City." She turned to me. "You're so much more graceful than the rest of our family."

"I don't know about that; Mom's a good dancer."

"Psh, she's nothing compared to you."

I smiled at her. Derek asked how long I'd be staying and I told him I was leaving Monday morning. Molly groaned.

"Well, we'll see about that," she muttered. "Oh, hey, do the thing!"

"What thing?"

"Les can read minds!" Molly said giddily to Derek.

"What?" Derek seemed almost scared.

"She's exaggerating," I spoke up. "Just think of a number."

"Um...okay."

"Forty-two."

Derek looked shocked. Molly laughed and clapped her hands like she was three. Honestly, though, I enjoyed it, too.

"Well, if you find yourself with free time tomorrow, we'll be doing a brief run-through starting at 5:00. You can come and watch if you want," Derek offered.

"Sure, I'd really like to see it. As long as Molly can give me a ride?"

"Yeah, don't worry about it. I'll drop you off before I go to work." Molly said nodding.

"Sounds like a plan! I'll see you tomorrow and we can talk more about New York," Derek beamed before we said good-bye.

As Molly and I left the theatre I caught sight of the non-existing woman. She was heading towards the stage door. I tried to get Molly's attention, but by the time we turned around she was gone.

"Cop's gone, we're in the clear," Jimmy tells me after disappearing for a few minutes to check the store. Jimmy buys a strawberry milkshake before we leave the Quick Check and again I ask Jimmy why he needed to see me.

"Les, that explosion was no accident."

"I don't doubt that—"

"But you don't seem to understand, man. That was meant to kill someone.... This non-existing existing woman, whoever she is, I don't think you can trust her."

"It was her house, Jimmy. Her stuff was there, her *cat*…. She's not going to blow up her own house."

"Then someone's trying to kill her, and you and your sister are smack in the middle of it all, whatever 'it' is."

"Why couldn't I bring my brother to hear this?"

"'Cause there's more." Jimmy stops walking. I stop too.

"There weren't just pictures of you in the house."

"Okay…. What, were there pictures of Danny?"

"Kinda," Jimmy takes something out of his pocket and gives it to me.

It's a picture of Danny from some birthday party when we were teenagers. Jimmy tells me to flip it over. I do and see there's writing on the back—a street address.

"It might be nothing," Jimmy starts to say, but I cut him off.

"This is Danny's address," I notice my hand's quivering.

"Yeah? See, I didn't want to worry him…. Les, does someone have something against your family?" Jimmy asks quietly. I can't answer. I can't imagine why anyone would want to hurt my family.

"That's not it," a voice responds to my thoughts. I look up. Scott's back.

"Ugh," I mutter aloud.

"Just hear me out," Scott says hurriedly. "Listen, don't be fooled by the way things look."

"Shut up. Leave me alone. You're not even real," I yell at him. Jimmy's confused and looks concerned, but I'm focused on Scott.

"You're right." Scott responds. "I'm just a part of you. That's why you should listen to me."

I'm quiet. He waits for me to say something. I don't, so he continues.

"I am your instinct, your inner thought, and I have never failed you. Face it; you need me right now. We can figure this out.... *You* can figure this out. Just let me help you. It's always good to have another, outside— or, maybe in this case, inside perspective on things."

Maybe he has something there. What did he know— what did *I* know—that I wasn't putting together?

"LES!" I realize Jimmy's trying to get my attention.

"It's not real! Whoever or whatever it is, it's not real."

I look back and forth between Scott and Jimmy. I realize I'm getting worse and sigh.

I'm sorry Scott, but I can't do this, I think to myself. "I'm gonna start taking the medication," I say out loud.

"What?! Fine, just...here!" Scott grabs my arm and pushes something in my hand. I swear I can feel it, a thick piece of paper in my hand. I look at it and see it's a playing card with an empty front. In the blank space there's a number written in small cursive: Thirty-two. I look up.

"Thirty-two?"

Scott shakes his head no, disappointed. I look back down at my hand but the card's gone, as is Scott.

"So, what are you thinking?" Jimmy's asking me.

I close my empty hand and put the photo of Danny in my pocket.

"I think…I think there's more to this than there appears to be.…"

I look Jimmy in the eyes and say confidently, "I don't think we have to worry about Danny. Let's just focus on finding Molly."

My cell phone rings. I pick it up and hear Brendan's voice.

"The woman you were looking for is here," the voice says.

"But you can't leave! I hardly spent any time with you!" Molly moaned. It was already Sunday and I was attempting to pack. It was proving to be a difficult task. Molly sat on my suitcase, grabbed the clothes I had in my hands, and held them behind her back.

"There's this great party we could go to tomorrow night, and I'm completely free all Tuesday morning!"

"Get off or I'll tickle you."

"I'll pay for your drinks? Listen to me! Ever since you left for New York I hardly ever see you!"

"I know I'm irresistible, but—"

"Les." Molly looked serious. Her eyes drooped and she gave me a pitiful, sad puppy-dog look. I sighed to myself. My brothers were never this clingy.

I reviewed my schedule in my head and realized I actually was free until the end of the month, but never considered staying in Jersey for that long.

"Please?"

"Maybe…I'll call Jenny and ask if I could come

back Wednesday instead."

"Thank you! See, I knew you couldn't resist my puppy eyes."

"Yeah, well, it's more pathetic than cute."

"Whatever works!" she said cheerfully. "So, am I dropping you off at the theatre?"

"Sure. I'm excited about this play—it'll also be interesting to see how good of an actor Derek is."

It's sunset when I get back to the theatre. The sky has turned into a water-color painting, a blend of blue and purple sky dotted with pink clouds. The sun hides behind the silhouettes of flourishing trees, and the air has a scent that can only be described as summer.

I see that Danny had called my cell phone about seven times. *He's going to kill me,* I think. I walk up the steps of the theatre and attempt to open one of the doors. It doesn't budge. I try all the other front doors, but each one is locked. Maybe the rehearsal ended already? I back up and examine the building. The air is still and silent and I feel oddly alone, like I'm the only human on the planet.

The rehearsal must be over. I didn't get here fast enough.

I walk back to Danny's car, look at the theatre again, and notice a side door to the building in the alley between the theatre and the neighboring Italian restaurant. That might be unlocked....

I walk over and find the door propped open. Inside the theatre is dark and empty. The curtains are closed, and the only light comes from the glowing red exit sign.

"Hello?" I call out.

Silence responds, telling me to abandon my quest and go back to the car. I'm not convinced. I move through the dark and scan every row to make sure the non-existing woman isn't hiding somewhere, watching me with that peculiar, almost sinister smile. I desperately hope she's here somewhere.... Right now she's the only thing connecting me to Molly.

I walk around for maybe ten minutes before I decide to leave. Then I notice a sliver of orange light escaping from underneath the door leading to the backstage office.

Someone *is* here.

I walk over and hear someone whispering inside. I creep closer to the door. Whoever it is, he/she is on the phone. The voice is so faint the conversation is hardly comprehensible, until suddenly the mystery person shouts, "Where the *hell* are you? Do you really think you can *hide* from me?!"

Is that my sister on the other line? The voice goes quiet again. I kneel down to the door and slowly press my ear to its chipping painted wood. It only helps slightly.

"You know I'd never hurt you...I told you, I have nothing to do with that, I don't know what happened! Maybe someone else knows. I mean, that would make sense, if they were after.... Of course you can trust me! I'm your best friend. For God's sake, stop being so overdramatic.... Don't...I said don't! I had no choice; you know that, you were there. We have to work together.... Yes.... Yes, I promise, we'll find the guy who did this. You know the cops think it was that psycho Leslie."

My breath gets caught in my throat. *They must be talking about the explosion.* The conversation gets quiet again.

"Can we talk? Face to face, I mean?"

I could feel the conversation coming to an end. I slowly back away from the door, listening to the person pace inside.

LIGHT! A sudden explosion of it nearly gives me a heart attack. The stage lights are suddenly on, brightly lighting the foreboding red curtains. I stumble back, making a scuffling noise. The person on the phone goes quiet.

"Someone's here...." I could faintly hear the person whisper.

I need to hide.... I dash for the stage, fumble around to find an opening and hide behind the curtains. I hear the light in the office click off and the door creak open. Then nothing...I strain to hear footsteps when I feel a gust of wind behind me. I turn around to see the lit set and am shocked.

An exact replica of the unknown woman's bedroom stands before me. I stare at it, expecting it to change back into the surrealistic set my brother and the crew had been building and walking around all week.

"This...this is impossible," I whisper to myself.

I venture closer to the set. Every detail of the room

is as it was the night of the explosion. The black cat covers on the bed, the fan that's on yet again, the pictures of me scattered all over the bed and floor—as if I'd walked into the past.

My shaky hand turns off the fan. I look around at the pictures on the floor and see the one of my brother at the birthday party.... *But....*

I search my pockets and pull out the exact same photo with Danny's address written on the back.

Okay, calm down.... I take a deep breath. Then I realize what this is.

I turn around but the theatre curtain is gone, replaced by a bedroom wall. I'm trapped in the vivid memory of the non-existing woman's room. I look back at the floor at the photograph of my brother.

"I'm imagining this.... This isn't real," I say slowly. Nothing changes. *Great, I'm stuck in a hallucination.*

I remember what Scott said. *Maybe he was right.... Maybe I missed something? Maybe I'm seeing this again because there's something here worth noticing, something I overlooked?*

"Bingo," I hear. Scott stands beside me. "Look around. Closet full of clothes. The bed's made. The fan and lights are on. There's a credit card on the desk, and there's still smoke rising from the cigarette in the ashtray. Does it look like she planned for this house to blow up?" Scott asks. I shake my head.

"Remember what you see here," he tells me.

I look around the room again, paying close attention to everything I see. The bed's made but the rest of the room's a mess. If she's a messy person, why would she make her bed? Why *are* the photos scattered everywhere? From the fan and smoking cigarette I could tell she was waiting for me. But when she left she didn't grab her credit card.... Or her cat.

"Was there lipstick on the cigarette?" Scott asks me.

"Um.... No," I remember.

"She does wear lipstick, right?"

"Yeah.... So the cigarette wasn't hers."

"And the mess? The pictures?" Scott asks as he circles me, getting my mind working.

"Someone was looking for something.... A photo," I look down at the picture in my hand. "Maybe the one with Danny's address?"

"The card." Scott says, pointing to the playing card face down on the bed. I go over and pick it up, but it isn't the Queen of Diamonds this time. Instead there's a number in the center, written in cracked cursive: 38. I look up at Scott. Scott sighs and shakes his head.

"What does this mean?" I ask roughly, but Scott runs past me. I turn around and suddenly everything is pitch black, *silent*. The lights are off. I wave my arms in front of me and feel the theatre curtain. I grab it and pull it over to find the opening. While my eyes are trying to adjust I manage to catch a glimpse of someone running out the side door of the theatre. I'm not sure, but...I think it looked like Brendan.

"I'm sorry that, yet again, I'll be leaving you by yourself tonight," Molly said to me as I got out of the car.

"Hey, don't worry about it. Anyway, I'm sure I'll see Danny in there managing props, so I'll have a ride home."

"Wait, wait, Les! What color am I thinking of?"

"Green."

"You're a freak."

We waved good-bye, I closed the car door, and Molly drove off, leaving me in front of the theatre. I headed towards the building and found a familiar woman leaning against the theatre door, smoking a cigarette.

"What card am I thinking of?"

"Queen of Diamonds again?"

The non-existing woman smiled and blew some smoke in my face, then said, "Leslie; interesting name."

"What...how...?"

"Brendan told me. You're Danny's brother?"

"Yep."

"So theatre runs in the family?"

"Well, I'm more dance-concentrated than theatre."

She blew more smoke in my face and I started to cough.

"Not a smoker, are you?" she asked wistfully.

"You...*cough*...caught that?"

"Of course you're not a smoker." She moved the cigarette to the side of her mouth. Her now free hands grasped my upper arms.

"You're a dancer.... You keep your body healthy." Her hands moved from my biceps to my chest. I watched her, stunned, unsure what to do.

"You're also in great shape," she continued. Her

fingers crossed down to my abs and I stopped her hands there, before they had a chance to move any…lower.…

"You should wear tighter clothes," she said, looking up at me as if what she was doing was perfectly normal. I slowly took her hands away from my stomach.

"Well, I'll keep that in mind."

"Such a shame," she sighed.

"What is?"

She suddenly pulled her hands out of mine, grabbed the cigarette, and blew yet more white suffocation at me.

"I have to go. I have a purchase to make," she said shortly before turning on her black heels and walking briskly away down the sidewalk. I watched her leave, thinking again how bizarre she was. I was growing more and more fond of her.

"Danny, please, let me explain." I attempt to calm my brother, but he's impossible; pacing the apartment, screaming at me, just like I knew he would.

"You're under my custody, Les! What you did, taking off like that, was *illegal*!"

"Jimmy called; he said it was important—"

"What if some cop saw you? You'd be thrown in jail if not a mental institution, and people—you are sane, Les, although you're beginning to prove otherwise—sane people don't do well in mental institutions!"

"Jimmy found a clue from the house. Listen, I wouldn't have gone if I didn't think it was important."

"I called you, like, eighty times. I could've sworn you picked up once and hung up on me, which pisses me off, by the way, but that aside, I'm in charge of you, you're *my* responsibility. I could've been arrested for letting you out of my sight!"

"I went back to the theatre after Brendan called, but by the time I got there, the rehearsal was already over."

"And you stole my car. I can *kill* you for that—I will kill you for that! When you die, it will be my fault," Danny stops his ranting and turns to me. "There was no rehearsal tonight."

"So I discovered."

"Who's this Brendan?"

"I met him at the theatre, when I sat in on one of the rehearsals. He's an understudy, wears a lot of *42ⁿᵈ Street* merchandise, today it was a hat?"

"Yeah, okay, whatever. Why did he tell you there was a rehearsal?"

"I don't know, but when I got to the theatre he was talking to someone on the phone. He knows about the explosion."

Danny's thinking. He starts pacing back and forth in front of me.

"What did he say?"

"I don't remember exactly, but it sounded like he was talking to that woman, the Queen of Diamonds."

"Are you sure it was him?"

"I don't know for sure, but I saw him running out of the theatre. I mean, there might have been someone else there turning on and off lights."

"What, like, stage lights?"

"Yeah, but no…I thought.…"

"What are you talking about?"

"Well, I'm not sure if I really saw it, or thought I saw it...." I try to explain without saying out and out "I may have imagined everything". Unfortunately, Danny knows me too well.

"What do you *think* you saw?" Danny asks slowly, his eyes narrowing.

"Uh, the lights turned on and the curtains opened, and, uh.... Then I was in that woman's bedroom."

"The one that exploded?"

I nod slightly and, looking down, quietly add, "Scott was there."

I don't want to see Danny's expression. I keep my eyes low as he marches angrily past me and grabs something from the kitchen. He returns and forces a bottle of pills in my hand.

"I'm not taking—" I start. He cuts me off.

"Stop. Just…just take them." Danny puts a cup of water in my other hand. I glance up at him and wish I hadn't. I've never seen him so mad. I feel like a little kid being scolded and punished as I put the pills in my mouth. My throat refuses to swallow the little white capsules, but the water smooths it out and the pills slip down. They leave a plastic-y, unpleasant taste in my mouth. I hand back the cup of water and the bottle and feel a sense of defeat.

Danny puts a hand on my shoulder. Now I refuse to look at him out of spite.

"Les, I'm sorry, but Mark's right. We can't be worrying about you every second and at the same time manage a search party for Molly.…"

I think he wants me to say something. I don't. He continues.

"Well, *mi casa es su casa*. Make yourself comfortable; you know where the guest bedroom is."

I start to head for the room but he grabs my arm.

"Listen, I know you're mad at me, but if something happens tonight—like, some allergic reaction or side effect from the medication, or you feel sick or something—tell me, okay?"

I sigh. He hasn't let go of my arm yet, and I realize he's waiting for me (forcing me) to respond.

"Yeah, okay," I say out loud. He lets go and I retire to the guest bedroom.

I lie on the bed and feel blank. My mind is bare. Lately I've been thinking a lot about Molly. Where could she be? Is she okay? What's going on?

But not tonight. Tonight I feel empty. Knowing I have some sort of chemicals rushing through my system makes me feel…different. Crazier than when I wasn't on medication.

Throughout the night I'm twitching and searching the room, positive I heard a sound or voice. I was told the medication takes a few days before it starts working. So perhaps it's all psychological; I've tricked myself into believing the medication makes me worse when, in fact, it's beneficial to my mental health.

But then I realize that's what scares me. The idea that medication would somehow change me. I'd be alone; on medication, I'd never see Scott again. He wouldn't be there to help me find Molly. I'd also never have to question whether or not something's real, and for some reason that just didn't seem like me.

I close my eyes but can't sleep. I think of sheep, count backwards from a hundred, let my mind wonder. Eventually I look at the clock. It's already 3:00—this will be the forth night in a row I'll be getting less than five hours of sleep, if I get any at all. *Wonderful.*

Pick up, pick up, pick up....

"Hello?"

"Jenny! Thank god you're home."

"Hey, Les! What's up, something wrong? You sound out of breath."

"Okay, Jenny, you, you aren't going to believe the night I just had."

"Something interesting?"

"Interesting is putting it mildly!"

I had just returned from hanging out with Jimmy at the bar (admittedly drunk) and was eager to tell Jenny all about the robbery at Quick Check. I delved into the story, stammering a bit, and waited for her reaction. When I finished she asked the two questions I knew she would.

"That really happened? Wow.... I mean, are you sure this Jimmy guy is real?"

The second question bummed me out, of course, because at the time I had to honestly answer "No".

"I don't think I imagined it," I told Jenny. "I've had my moments, but this, this was crazy, this was far too complicated and involved too many people to be entirely fake. Plus, I'm sure Molly saw him at the party the first time we met."

"Well, ask her. Next time you see her, ask. Did you tell her the story yet?"

"No, I just got home. You were the first person I called."

"Okay, well, ask her before you tell her the story. God, I wish I was there. I should've gone with you, I'm missing out on way too much."

"So you're saying you *want* to be taken hostage during a robbery at gunpoint?"

"You had a great time, didn't you?"

"I wouldn't put it quite like that, but—"

Jenny suddenly gasped.

"What? What's wrong?"

Jenny hesitated before saying "Um, never mind. I'm probably wrong anyway."

"What? What were you going to say?"

"Uh...I don't know, I just thought of something.... You remember that robbery that went wrong—the one you told me about, where your psychologist was killed?"

"Yeah?"

"I just...I don't know.... I just think it's a strange coincidence. I mean, you visit your home town—a boring, quiet little place that's always been very safe—and you meet this kid Jimmy who robs stores with a gun right after your psychologist was murdered during a robbery in the same area."

"What are you suggesting?"

"Nothing! I just.… You sure this Jimmy guy can be trusted? I mean, he seems like the perfect suspect of that other robbery—"

"No. I can tell; Jimmy wouldn't hurt a fly."

"Well, just, do me a favor and stay away from him, okay? I don't want something bad to happen to you," I was a little surprised to hear Jenny say. I wanted to shrug off her warning, but the concern in her voice gave impact to her words. But she didn't know Jimmy. Jimmy wasn't dangerous.… I didn't think so, at least.

I watch as night turns to day with a dread in my heart. I didn't get any sleep. I didn't do anything constructive. I don't feel like myself right now, and this not-me has to attend a psychological evaluation and therapy session today, conducted by some stranger who probably believes that I'm guilty of blowing up that house. I didn't do anything but put myself in danger to find my sister.

Time speeds up and slows down in my state of insomnia, and before I know it I'm sitting in front of Dr. Bandos—the psychologist working with my lawyer. Her office, though big, is disturbingly intimate with the furniture pushed close together in the center of the room. I wouldn't ordinarily mind being so close to someone else, but unlike the people you sit next to on the subway or brush by on the sidewalk, this woman is here to study my every move and record my every thought, trying to decide whether or not I'm crazy enough to lock up. That my freedom's fate rests in this stranger's hands isn't a pleasant thought.

"How are you feeling today, Mr. Adams?" she begins. I tell her to call me "Les". This causes her to scribble something much longer than the three-letter name down on her pad of paper. When she's finished, she looks back up at me and asks another question.

"Have you been taking your medication?"

So we've already skipped the chit-chat.

"Yes." I say flatly.

"How are you reacting to it?"

Like you care, as long as it works.

"I couldn't sleep. I don't think it works."

"Well, once it gets into your system it should start working. In a week, if you still have sleeping problems, let me know and we'll—"

"I'm not crazy."

She raises her eyebrows.

"I mean, I don't think I need medication."

"Why do you think that?"

"I'm sure I can manage just fine without them. I've done fine without any sort of medication all my life. I know what's real and what isn't."

"Mmm-hmm." She goes back to writing in her notepad. "All right. Let's talk about the night of the fire. How did you get to the house?" she asks, still looking down at her writing.

I want to take that pad and throw it out the window.

"I was told to go there. Someone gave me the address—"

"The non-existing woman?"

How did she know that?

She answers my confused expression with a contemplated, "You told me when you were under hypnosis."

"She exists.... I just don't know her name, that's all."

More scribbling. *What could she possibly be scribbling?*

"So, what did this woman tell you? Did she tell you to meet her at that house specifically?"

"Yes."

"Why?"

"She said she had information I needed."

"What information?"

It's getting harder and harder to avoid bringing up Molly's disappearance. I don't want to tell this woman that Molly's missing, but with how things are playing out I might not have a choice.

"Tell me the truth, Leslie. Either I get this information straight from you now, or I'll extract it later during hypnosis."

"You need my consent to perform hypnosis."

"You're the prime suspect in a serious crime; things change in these kinds of situations."

That sounded like a threat. I'm not liking the way this session is going. Maybe I should just tell her about Molly.

"Do I have your promise of doctor-patient confidentiality?" I ask hesitantly.

"Depends on what you tell me. If it's information that directly proves you're guilty, I have to tell your lawyer. If it's something that involves hurting others or hurting yourself, I must take further action."

"What about gray areas?"

My psychologist keeps her expression blank but I could see the intrigue in her eyes. I continue.

"It doesn't exactly have to do with this case and no one's getting hurt, but the police would probably be interested."

"Does it have to do with why you were at the house?"

I nod, reading every change in her expression, trying to read her mind. I'm unsuccessful, of course.

"I can't make any promises...." She fiddles with her pen for a second, then smiles. "But you can trust that I only want to help you."

I regard her like a dog would of a stranger with a squeaky toy, weighing my options.

"She called me—the non-existing woman. I don't know how she got my number."

I start to tell her what I remember...

"Hello?"

"Les."

"Who is this?"

"Queen of Diamonds."

"Good-bye—"

"Wait, wait, wait!"

It was the fourth time I've been in contact with the non-existing woman. The third encounter I'll discuss later.

"You're not real," I tell the non-existing woman.

"I know about Molly."

Silence.

"I know what happened to her and why. I also have

information concerning your family…concerning you. Please, come see me."

"How do you know about Molly?"

"I'll explain everything later, just meet me.… Come to my house."

"Is she okay? Where is she?"

"I can't talk; he might be nearby."

"Who?"

"The Queen of Diamonds."

"*What?*"

"201 Evergreen Road, purple house. See me *tonight.*"

"Wait—"

She hung up, leaving me lost and confused.

"Who was that?" Jimmy asked. He and Danny were with me, combing Molly's apartment for clues.

"The non-existing woman."

Danny's attention snapped to me.

"Wait! Wait, wait, wait—" he jumped across the room over Molly's litter of clothes and books to me, grabbed me, and shook me harder than he probably meant to.

"Who called? Who really called?"

"The non-existing woman, now let go of me—"

"She's called 'non-existing' for a reason. She isn't real, Les! She's a figment of your imagination!"

"I'm not so sure about that."

"Yeah, come on, dude, we all heard the phone ring," Jimmy said to Danny, backing me up. Danny looked annoyed. He let go of me, glared at Jimmy, and left the room. I watched him go, then slid over to Jimmy.

"She told me to meet her," I whispered to him. "If you could...I mean, it'd be helpful if...."

"Sure, I'll go with you. Count me in," Jimmy whispered back.

"I'm not sure about this."

"Don't worry. I'll bring...." Jimmy made a gun with his hand. "Protection."

"I don't think we'll need anything like that—"

"Les, I don't plan to use it. It's just for the worst-case scenario. You can't take this situation too lightly; your sister is missing—"

"Yeah, okay, I just...I don't have a good feeling about this."

"Your sister is missing?" my psychologist asks.

"Yes. At least, we think so."

"Why haven't you contacted the police?"

"Because she might have disappeared on purpose. You can't tell the police that she's gone either," I say, looking her straight in the eyes. She looks back at me, not a change in her expression. We look at each other for a while before she changes the subject.

"So the gun wasn't yours?"

"I don't want Jimmy to get into any trouble. If keeping him out of trouble means the gun has to be mine instead of his, then the gun is mine."

"Stop worrying about Jimmy. You're the one in trouble."

I sigh and glance at the clock. Hopefully this session won't go on for too much longer. I can't take much more of this.

"Hello?"

"Hey Les, I'm sorry, I won't be coming home tonight," Molly's voice told me.

"What? Not at all?" This disappearing act of Molly's was getting old. It was Tuesday, I was going to leave the next day as Molly had convinced me, and I hadn't seen any more of her than before.

"No. You know my roommate Trish? She has something important to tell me. I'm heading over to her mother's house now."

"How's that going to take all night?"

"Listen, I can't really explain. I'll catch up with you tomorrow. Call Danny and get a ride to the theatre tomorrow morning, I'll see if I can meet you there."

"Wait, why don't you just meet me here?"

"We can't talk in the apartment."

What?

"Molly, what's going on?"

She stuttered, then, "I can't talk, I'm driving. You know, it'd be really helpful if you went shopping for me. The shopping list is on the fridge."

"How can I go shopping if I don't have a car?" I snapped.

"There's a Quick Check just down the street, I'm sure it'll have what we need. I gotta go—"

"Wait, wait! Someone called for you a while ago, called back again today. Did you buy a ticket to Hawaii on your credit card?"

"What?"

"I don't know, you tell me. She said your flight has

been overbooked; they're putting you on a later flight or something. They said it was paid with your card."

"Shit. You know what, my credit card was stolen a few days ago, I forgot to cancel it! Shit, thanks for reminding me. I'll see you tomorrow, okay?"

"Fine."

"Don't be mad at me."

"I'm not! I'll just.... I'll go get the stuff on your shopping list."

"Thanks, bye!"

"Bye...."

After my psychiatric session, Danny and I stop off at Molly's apartment to get my luggage.

"I have to meet with this freakin' doctor same time tomorrow. She wants to do more hypnosis," I tell Danny.

"I think that's a good idea," Danny says, throwing a handful of clothes into my suitcase.

"What?!"

"I think she could help you figure out what's real and what's not."

"I know what's real."

I catch Danny rolling his eyes. "So the meds gave you a hard time last night?"

"Why you think that?"

"Well, it would explain the sour attitude."

I pick up a T-shirt and try to figure out if it's mine or Molly's.

"Hey, I know what will make you feel better!"

"Really?" I scoff at the idea.

"Yeah. I've got a key to the theatre. There's no one there now, and the stage is pretty cleared out, so, you know."

"What are you driving at?"

"You can go dance. Get everything out, calm down, let go of that stress and anger and whatever you're bottling up. I can even bring music, if you want. What kind of thing do you dance to? Bach or Gaga?"

"Let me guess; you have a lot of Gaga, don't you?"

"Just got her new CD!"

"You're *so* gay."

"Hey, don't dis Gaga."

I smile and imagine an empty stage.

"I should probably practice…fine. Let me just change clothes first."

"Okay. I'll meet you downstairs in the car, all right?"

"Yeah." I shuffle through the bundle of clothing in my suitcase, trying to find some flexible pants. I decide against making Danny wait—I'll just change at the theatre.

I grab some black sweats, run over to the door, and just stop myself from smashing into Trish. As surprised as I am to see her, she seems more surprised to see me.

"Les! Hey, what are you—"

"Where's Molly?" I demand.

"What?"

I grab her, pull her into the room and slam the door closed.

"WHERE'S MOLLY?!" I yell at her, faking anger I should but don't really have. She sits on the couch and starts playing with a few blonde strands of hair.

"What are you talking about?"

"You know what I'm talking about!"

"Uh, no, I don't."

"Last Tuesday, Molly went to your house to talk to you about something important, what was it?"

"I'm sorry, I don't remember."

Now I really am getting angry.

"You don't remember?"

Trish is looking more and more uncomfortable. She sighs and stands up.

"Um, I gotta go somewhere. Maybe she was talking to someone else on Tuesday."

I watch her leave, realizing she really has no idea what I'm talking about. *What if Molly never made it to Trish's house?* Then I remember that wasn't the last time I heard from Molly before she disappeared. I'm confused; none of this is making sense, and the sound of Danny honking his car horn interrupts any comprehensible thought. *I'll worry about all of this later. I need to clear my mind.*

It was pouring. The sky was dark. Heavy clouds covered the atmosphere, creating so much gray it was hard to believe the sky's true color lay hidden beneath, a pretty light blue somewhere beyond.

It was miserable weather. What made it more miserable was being forced to walk around outside without a raincoat. By the time I got to the theatre, my hoodie was so soaked it looked like I'd jumped into a pool.

I ran up the theatre steps and stood shivering under

the awning, disgusted with how cold and clingy my clothes were. My hair hung down in front of my face and my teeth were chattering.

FLASH. I realized the light wasn't lightning, but the flash from a camera. I looked next to me and saw the non-existing woman standing there, a cigarette in her mouth, a camera in her hands, smiling at me again. The Polaroid camera spat out a photo. She grabbed it and immediately started to shake it, letting the camera hang around her neck, swinging slightly. She watched the photo develop and laughed.

"Cute picture," she said smoothly, stuffing the photo in my face. I looked like a wet cat.

"Well, *I* like it," she said in reaction to my disgusted expression. "It will go great with the rest of my collection."

"What collection?"

"It's entitled 'The Many Faces of Leslie Adams'."

"Is that right?"

"Be flattered."

"Oh, I am."

She bit her bottom lip, as if trying to make up her mind whether or not to tell me something. That made me curious. She sighed and looked at the picture as she said, "You should get out of here."

"Back out in that rain? No thanks. Anyway, I'm looking for Molly, my sister—"

"She's not here."

"Uh, do you even know who she is?"

"I don't mean get out from under the awning, I mean

get out of New Jersey." She looked up at me, her eyes, outlined black with eyeliner, large and almost worried.

"Why?" I ask, taking her seriously now.

"You know you ask a lot of questions?"

I was tempted to say "What?" She went back to smoking and looked off into the rain. She wouldn't say another word.

I enter the theatre. Danny was right, the place is empty. I throw down my stuff onto a chair in the first row and go to chan—WAIT! What happened then? There was more….

I was about to enter the theatre when the non-existing woman grabbed my shoulder.

"Beware Brendan.… But I didn't say anything."

I looked at her, confused. She put a finger to her lips. Then, keeping her eyes glued to me, she opened the door of the theatre and waved her hand, ushering me in. She pushed the door closed behind me after I entered, and if it wasn't for the warmth in the theatre, I would've gone back out to talk with her more.…

I should have. Beware Brendan. Did she have something against him, or was there something else? Now I wonder if she was suggesting to me that Brendan had something to do with Molly's disappearance.

Music starts and it stops my thoughts dead. I'm back in the theatre. It's not raining out. Danny's with me, but otherwise the theatre's empty. I listen to the music and am glad Danny hadn't put on Gaga. Instead, a cool, rhythmic jazz, a deep blues piece, floats through the air. I climb up on the stage and warm up, stretching and bending. In the front row I can hear my brother grunt his annoyance with my flexibility.

"You're going to live to be a hundred, aren't you?" He shouts at me.

"Here," I tell him, handing him my iPod. I point out a song and take my place center-stage. The jazz stops and the classical piece I've danced to over and over again starts to play. I take a deep, slow breath and the theatre slips away. I disappear into a world of strings and soft piano which dictate my inhale and exhale.

I start to rehearse and feel like I'm back in NYC. I can see my beautiful young dance partner in her silky white dress, gracefully spinning, her face placid. The stress is disappearing from my body and my mind feels released of a burden, clearer and more able. I completely lose track of time.

Eventually I hear the end of the song approach. The strings are loud and frantic. Quick movements, little breathing. The music builds up and abruptly stops. End position. Fade to black. House lights up. Time to leave the stage.

I realize someone's clapping and look down at the sea of chairs. The theatre has just now reappeared. I see my brother smiling at me, and next to him, out of his seat, Jimmy is clapping wildly.

"Wow…. Just, wow, man! You're a professional! Well, you *are* a professional, but I mean, you're good. I'm not even into this theatre stuff, but that was—"

"When did you get here?"

"I've been here for a while now, actually. I said hi

and stuff, but Danny said you wouldn't hear me."

"I told you," my brother says smugly. "Once he gets on stage, he's in another world. Isn't that right, Les? You looked good, by the way."

"You only saw half. The piece is a duet." I'm suddenly thinking of my sister again. I shake away my worry and turn to Jimmy. "How did you know we'd be here?"

"I called your cell, Danny picked up and told me you were here.… Why, are you mad at me or something?"

"No," I say honestly, jumping off stage and grabbing my change of clean clothes. I'm not mad, just thoughtful. I'm realizing now how many warnings I've been getting lately. Jenny says stay away from Jimmy, and Danny and Mark seem to feel the same way. The four of them don't think I can trust the non-existing woman, and she told me I should beware of Brendan. And yet not Jimmy, the non-existing woman, nor Brendan seemed dangerous to me.

"I just need to think," I say to myself, sitting down in a chair. I hold my head in my hands and ruffle my hair, then notice something lying on the ground.

"Okay, Les, come on. We gotta put the set back the way it was. Hey Jimmy, can you grab those props— No, no, not those, the suitcases; just bring them over here."

"Oh my god, what did you put in these? Rocks?" Jimmy complains, dragging a suitcase across the stage.

"Don't be such a wuss—"

"Hey, guys," I interrupt. I pick up the leather-bound notebook and raise it up for them to see.

"Is this either of yours?"

"Do I look like I keep a journal?" Jimmy scoffs.

Danny shrugs. "Not mine."

I look at the journal and flip it open to the first page to check for a name.

"Hey, Danny, has Mark ever been here? To the theatre?"

"Maybe once a while ago."

"Then this must be Molly's."

"What?" Jimmy and Danny say simultaneously. Jimmy drops the suitcase with a thud and jumps down from the stage. Danny follows him. On the first page of the notebook is a place to write the journal owner's name. The person only put their last name: Adams.

"She didn't write her name, but Molly used to keep a journal in high school.... I mean, I think we can trust this isn't Mom or Dad's," I say slowly, starting to flip through the pages. Jimmy looks uncomfortable.

"If that's her diary.... I mean, you're not going to read it, are you?"

Danny and I look at each other.

"Uh, hell yeah!" Danny answers for me.

"Also like in high school.... Anyway, it might give us hints as to why she's gone," I add, still flipping through the pages. I stop at one that catches my interest. There's just one sentence written in the center of the page, surrounded by drawings of diamonds and rings. It reads two simple words: "I'm rich!"

"Hey, Derek, have you seen Molly?"

"Hi, Les. You mean today?"

"Yeah." I jumped up and sat next to him on the edge of the stage. He looked me up and down and smiled. "I guess it's raining."

"Yeah," I laughed. I looked down and realized I was dripping all over the stage.

"Um, no, haven't seen her today. Were you planning to meet her here or something?"

"Yeah, she called me last night, said she'd be here."

"Sorry. Hope you have a ride back."

"Nope. If she doesn't show, I'll have to walk back home in the rain."

"Well, stick around for a while. Danny might show up; he could give a ride home."

"Good thinking," I told him. I looked down at the script he had in his hand. He moved it so I could see it better.

"Hey," I hesitated. I looked up, just to check if Brendan was around. He wasn't. "Do you know Brendan?"

Derek's eyes darted from the paper up to me. He seemed frozen for a moment, then raised his eyebrows. "Who?"

"He's an actor here, I think. You know him?"

"Why?" he asked quickly.

"Someone told me to stay away from him. I'm trying to figure out why," I said slowly.

"Who? Who said…?"

Derek stopped after seeing my expression. He eased up and laughed. "Sorry, I'm just…. See, whoever it was is probably being overdramatic. There are so many people in the production getting together and breaking up and backstabbing each other, and.… Well, I'm a bit of a gossip queen, myself. You know theatre folk.…"

I did. Dancers can get rather caddy; most of my friends thrived on conflict and gossip. But it was obvious Derek wasn't telling me something.

"I know the type," I said aloud. "So, do you know this guy? Brendan?"

"Nope."

"No?"

"Haven't even heard of him. Sorry.…"

Someone stole Jimmy's car. He couldn't be happier.

"Are you sure someone stole it?" Danny says, walking around the lot in circles.

"Yeah," I add, "I find it hard to believe that anyone would want to steal that piece of junk. Maybe it was just towed?"

"Nope!" Jimmy shouts happily, skipping around the parking lot. "No, it was right here! I left it here, and now it's gone! You guys, this is great! Me and the boys, we've been trying to figure out what to do with that piece of shit for a while now. I mean, since that was our get-away car, that's incriminating evidence. Also, it was just a matter of time before that yellow deathtrap got pulled over. I guess you guys will just have to give me a lift!" Jimmy comes to a halt next to my brother who gives him a painful smile.

"Sure," Danny says through clenched teeth.

On our way to drop off Jimmy I look through my phone for missed messages. There are two. The first one's from Jimmy, asking where we are. Danny must've picked up the second time he called. I delete it, skip to the second message which is apparently a day old.

"8:25 p.m.," the electric voice introduces. It was when I was driving back to the theatre yesterday. My phone beeps and the message begins.

"Les, it's Molly."

"WHAT?!" I scream so loud my brother swerves and the phone flies out of my hand. I dive over Jimmy, trying to catch the phone.

Danny pulls off to the side of the road looking terrified, Jimmy's leaning back in his seat looking confused and uncomfortable, and I must look insane, scrambling to get a grip on the phone, which has decided to seize this opportunity to escape. I'm stretched across Jimmy's lap by the time I finally get a hold of it. I franticly fiddle with the buttons, restart the message, and yell at Danny (who's yelling at me) to be quiet.

"Les, it's Molly," my sister's shaky voice repeats. "I was really hoping you'd pick up, but…uh…listen, don't worry about me. I'm fine, I'm okay, but you have to go back to New York City, all right? Just leave, take Mark and Danny with you, too, okay? This is important, Les. You have to—BEEP. End of messages."

"Wh-What?" I stutter. *Beep? Why beep?* Did she get cut off or did someone cut her off, or maybe her cell went dead or—*Oh no.…* I check the settings on my phone. *Did my answering machine cut her off early?*

"Les, what the hell?!"

No, no, no, what was she going to say?

"Les? Les?!"

"Molly!"

"What?"

"Molly called me! She called last night and left a message...I...it.... The damn phone cut her off!"

"Give me that." Danny snatches the phone out of my hands. I watch his reaction as he listens to the message.

"Uh, hey, Les?" Jimmy asks quietly. "I, I know this is a big deal and all, but could you get off of me?"

I prop myself up and scramble into the front seat next to my brother. He's listening to the message a second time.

"So?" I ask when he's finished. He looks at the phone, then his expression turns bewildered. He looks at me, as if expecting me to say something comforting.... I hate being the oldest.

"Molly's okay," I say, faking confidence. I'm not sure how to respond to what Danny says next.

"What about us?"

"Hello?"

"Molly!" I shouted into the phone. I was back outside in the rain, trying to hide from the crying sky under a hunched over little tree.

"I walked all the way to the theatre in the pouring rain, waited there for you until rehearsal ended and they kicked me out, and then I've been calling you for, like, ever—"

"Calm down."

"Molly, don't tell me—"

"You're upset. That's bad. Les, I thought you've

been exercising."

"Don't change the subject! Molly, you have no idea the kind of shit you put me through by asking me to go grocery shopping for you last night. I'd go into it now, but honestly, I don't think you'd even believe me. You know the only reason I'm still in Jersey is because you *begged* me to stay, but then this whole time you haven't been around—okay, yes, I'm a bit worked up right now, but that's just because I've been standing in the goddamn rain all day, and hey, what the hell was so important that you couldn't even tell me over the phone last night?!"

Silence.

"Molly?"

"I don't know what you want me to say...are you at the apartment?"

"No, I'm in the rain."

"Good."

"What?"

"I'm sorry I've been so busy.... Maybe you should just go home."

Great, now she's upset. I sighed.

"I'm sorry for snapping at you. You know, it's just a really crappy day and I'm kinda hung over.... Also, I guess it's been a week since I—are you crying?"

"I love you, Les," Molly sobbed. That was a terrifying thing to hear.

"What the hell is going on, Molly? Are you okay? Where are you?" I started interrogating, but she cut me off with "I'm fine, I'm just...confused. Nothing's wrong, okay? I'm sorry I didn't meet you at the theatre."

"Molly—"

She hung up. I closed my phone and studied it, confused.

She's probably just PMS-ing, I'd thought. Then I never saw her again.

Night falls quick and eventually I find myself staring up at the ceiling, waiting to fall asleep again. I refused medication tonight, and while Danny seemed unhappy with my decision, he kept his mouth shut and kept the bottle out on the kitchen table. "Just in case you change your mind," he said.

I watch the ceiling fan spin in circles and wonder what Molly meant when she told me it was important for me to leave Jersey.

If only I could. Molly obviously hadn't heard about my little incident with the police. If it wasn't for this stupid tracking bracelet, I'd probably be taking Molly's advice right now.

My eyes are closed and little images, the beginnings of dreams, are flashing before me. I'm fighting them off, trying to concentrate on what Molly had said, but sleep is catching up to me quick and before long I'm down the rabbit hole.

I land on a coach in Dr. Patricia's mansion. Dust bursts out of the cushions, and when it finally settles I find I'm 10 all over again. Pre-teen Scott is flickering next to me, as if he's no more than a movie projection. The mansion is HUGE, like a child would imagine....

Vine-covered pillars stretch up from the shiny checkerboard floor, holding up a ceiling so high up, clouds block me from seeing where the walls end. The fireplace in the room looks like it's miles away, and yet the fire flickering within its stone cove is the only thing lighting the grand room.

I hop down from the couch and my footsteps echo as I come closer to the fireplace, leaving Scott behind. As I approach, a looming, harmonious little tune grows louder and more distinct and I wonder if I've heard this tune before. At last I reach the fireplace. Above it hangs a portrait of the late Dr. Patricia with the dates of her birth and death written in gold ink across the bottom. I turn to leave, ready to explore the rest of the mansion when a voice echoes loud and powerful through the empty palace, "You know who killed me." I turn around and find the portrait looking down at me, waiting expectantly.

"Wh-What?"

"You know who killed me."

I stare at the painting, my mouth agape. I'm not sure how to answer her, but before I could even ask her to clarify, Dr. Patricia's oil-painted hands reach out of the portrait. I watch, shocked, as she starts pulling herself out of her golden frame. I back up and fall into the coach, which has joined the two of us by the fireplace, and sit in silent awe as Dr. Patricia finishes prying herself from her canvas. She hops off the fireplace shelf onto the tiled floor, causing droplets of paint to splash all over.

I try to be polite and look her in the eyes, but can't help noticing she has no lower body. She seems just as surprised with this discovery as I am, but she doesn't let it bother her and looks up at me smiling.

"Hello, Les! How are you, sweetie?"

"Um.... You have no legs!" *10-year-old me points out.*

"And how does that make you feel, dear?"

Silence. I decide to ignore the question.

"You said I know who killed you?"

"Yes! Yes, and dear, they robbed me of everything! Those poor lost souls—"

"They? More then one?"

"Well, how should I know, Darling, you have the diary!"

"That diary's Molly's."

"All right."

"Molly didn't kill you."

"Oh, heavens no, of course not! I never said that."

"Then why did you bring up the diary?"

"Well, Molly is missing, I'm sure the diary will shed some light as to why."

"But what does that have to do with...."

Wait.... I rephrase my question.

"The people or person or whoever killed you.... Do they have something to do with Molly's disappearance?"

"Dear, do you like magic tricks?"

"Yes. I mean, what does that—"

"Pick a card!" *She spreads out a deck of cards*

which she seems to have pulled out of thin air. Since I'm 10 years old and easily distracted, I drop the topic of Molly's disappearance and gingerly pick a card. Queen of Diamonds; I should've known.

"My diamonds!" Dr. Patricia suddenly squeals. I look up at her, then back down at my hand and find that instead of holding a playing card, I'm holding a sparkling diamond necklace. The necklace...I remember this necklace. Dr. Patricia wore it during our sessions. But.... No, that must be a coincidence....

"The Queen is close, the Queen that killed me!" Dr. Patricia squeaks before jumping into the fire. I watch stunned as the fire eats her up and turns purple, then goes out. I'm in blackness. The musical tune starts up again, and a chill runs down my spine. I'm all alone, I'm 10, and I'm finding the eerie tune very unpleasant. Suddenly Scott jumps in front of me, screaming "SOME TWO QUEENS FLIPPED! MY GOD, DON'T YOU GET IT YET?!"

I wake up with a jolt, trying to catch my breath. I'm twenty-five again. I'm in Danny's guest bedroom. Everything's quiet. I lie back down on the bed and think of the dream.... What the hell kind of trippy dream was that? Some two Queens flipped? What the hell is that supposed to mean? It was some sort of riddle, obviously. For some stupid reason, my subconscious was making up riddles, even though I sucked at riddles— both figuring them out and, apparently, making them up.

I sit up and squeeze my head as if I can force the

answers out of it that way. Why couldn't it be something simple, like a picture? Maybe I should go back to sleep.

I fall back down on the bed again, get into a comfortable position, and wait to fall asleep. Of course, I've scared it off, and the stupid, incomprehensible little riddle keeps playing in my mind.

I have to clear my thoughts, relax, and drift, softly, gently, back to sleep...*sleep, god damn it, sleep!* I open my eyes and see the clock next to the bed. Half an hour has already passed. Is that possible? I couldn't have been lying here awake for that long.

Sleep, sleep, sleep.... Please sleep? Lack of sleep will drive a person crazy before his body shuts down completely. I'm already in a fragile state of mind, and for me sanity is getting harder and harder to come by these days.... Please, even if I don't dream, I just want to sleep. What time is it? *It's been an hour?* How is that possible? That's not fair.

I sit up again. Maybe the clock is broken? I wish that were true, but I doubt it. I look around the room, considering whether or not this is one of those nightmares about having insomnia. Then I remember the journal. I reach over the side of the bed and pick it up.

I open it and flip through the pages, waiting for something to pop out at me. Nothing specific does, so I just start to read a random page:

> She deserved it. There was no way of helping it anyway, no way around it. It's okay—a terrible waste, maybe. She was a good doctor....

But, then, no she wasn't. She failed me. She failed, it's her fault, she caused this it was all her fault she should have worked harder all her fault. All her fault. She didn't care.… She didn't care about me she didn't listen to me—she listened, she didn't hear, she didn't understand, she didn't care, she deserved it, she had it coming all her fault all her fault all her fault.

She didn't do anything for me, she didn't help me. She's evil. I was doing the world a favor; she was no good, a complete waste! A waste of schooling, a waste of money—she didn't *earn* all that shit, she was loaded, freakin' blissful in her wealth which she stole, she stole from me, from me and Trish.…

Trish? I read that again:

…She stole from me and Trish and everyone like us, we were just taking back what was rightfully ours. It was her fault we turned out this way, she did this to us, and all the people like her. Her fault, her bullshit questions and suggestions—'Find a hobby to focus your attention on,' stupid bullshit.

This wasn't Molly's journal.… This person was talking about Dr. Patricia. From the looks of it, it seemed like I found the diary of Dr. Patricia's murderer. "*Creepy*," I say out loud. I flip ahead a few pages and read some more. It becomes quite clear the journal wasn't written by any sane person. This belonged to a patient of Dr. Patricia, and whoever this person was, he or she knew Trish.

…Unless Molly was secretly psychotic and had gone to therapy and my parents never told me about it, but that seemed unlikely. I was the only one to ever attend therapy in our family, at least as far as I knew. Maybe I should ask Mom and Dad.…

I yawn and look at the time: 4:00 a.m. *Shit.*

The diary says "Adams." But that doesn't mean anything, Adams is a common last name.

My eyes are bugging out trying to read in the dark, so I put the journal away and look back up at the ceiling. I watch a blade of the ceiling fan spin in slow, hypnotic circles. My thoughts start to fade away.

Then one clear, creepy thought comes into my head. It's a wildly unrealistic idea, invented by a tired mind. But in this silent, dark room, it's gained power and pulled focus, and suddenly I can't think of anything else. I try to erase it from my mind, but like an itch it's impossible to ignore.…

Could that diary be mine?

"Calm down, Les! My god, did you run all the way here?"

"Aren't you listening to me? Molly's missing; she never came home, her cell phone's been disconnected—"

"I know, you told me over the phone. You didn't have to run here—"

"Danny, I'm serious."

"Shut up!" someone shouted from onstage. I looked up and realized the other actors had stopped rehearsing their scene and were staring at me. I grabbed Danny's arm and pulled him to the back of the theatre where we could talk without disturbing the actors.

"If you're hearing me, than why aren't you concerned?"

"I'm sure Molly's fine.… You seem emotional. You haven't danced in a while, have you?"

"No, I haven't. Yes, I know that's bad, Molly told me the same thing. But seriously, I haven't heard from her since yesterday and the things she was saying…I think there's something's wrong."

Danny smiled at me. Not the reaction I was expecting.

"Aw," he said. "Are you being an overprotective big brother?"

"Don't make me strangle you."

"I don't know what to tell you. I haven't seen her, sorry."

"Thanks, you're being very helpful. Where's Derek, maybe he's seen her."

"They aren't rehearsing his scene today; he's not here."

"Well, where is he?"

"I don't know."

"He's *your* boyfriend—"

"Yeah, I'm his *boyfriend*, not his mother. I'll ask him when I see him.… Which reminds me, did I tell you? You know that fancy new Japanese place on Sheelly Avenue? Derek's taking me there! Isn't that nice? It looks expensive, but Derek says—"

"Sounds nice, have you seen the woman in black?"

"What woman?"

"She's been here a few times. Has black wavy hair, kinda goth, a smoker, very pale white face, black eyes?"

"Black eyes?"

"Well, really, really dark brown, I guess, but they look black."

Danny became quiet. He looked around the theatre, than back at me.

"You saw her here?" he asked me.

"Three times, yeah. She was here yesterday, actually."

Danny looked worried. "How long has it been?"

"How long since I've seen her?"

"No, how long since you last danced?"

"What does that have to do with anything—"

"She doesn't exist."

"What?"

Danny grabbed me and pulled me closer to him and whispered "I know almost all the actors and crew members involved in this production, and none of them have black eyes—"

"Fine, not black! Just really, really dark brown. It's not that unusual—"

"You didn't think Scott's purple eyes were unusual either, remember?"

"Hey, wow, I was, like, seven, and this is different. I mean, why is that the first thing you jump to, that I'm seeing things?"

"Fine, has anyone else seen this woman?"

I stopped and tried to recall.

"Brendan did, I guess—"

"Was he with you when you saw her?"

"No."

"Was anyone with you any of the times you talked to her?"

Shit. "No."

"Did you see her wave to anyone or talk to anyone else—"

"No, all right? I guess...I mean, there's a possibility...." I looked up at Danny and stopped short. Danny avoided my gaze.

"Well," he said slowly, and then as if trying to compromise, "I can't be sure; you might be right, she may be real, in which case I just haven't met her. Just...I think you should get some exercise, okay?"

"What about Molly?"

"Hey, which suitcase am I supposed to be carrying right now?" an actor called to Danny from onstage. Danny started to walk away, being beckoned by the director.

"Listen," he called behind him. "Stick around tonight. Hang out in her apartment, keep calling. If she doesn't show up or pick up her phone, call me—or better yet, call Mark; I'll be on a date tonight!"

He flashed me a smile and gave me the thumbs up before jumping onstage to help the actors.

I can't sit still anymore. I jump out of bed and start to pace, swinging the diary around, almost afraid to look at it again.

I'm insane, but my condition is not that severe. I have psychosis, not multiple personality disorder. I haven't been sleeping at night, and I've been conscious of that, so there haven't been any gaps in my memory where I may have turned into someone else. Plus, nothing like this has ever happened to me before, certainly not in New York. *Oh, I really miss New York right now.* I miss the city and my dance company and Jenny and Bongo....

I look at the diary again. I'm not going to figure this out tonight, but before I place the book down on the nightstand two things come to mind. This can't be my diary because 1) this isn't my handwriting, and 2) more importantly, I don't know Trish. I've only bumped into her twice, and she didn't recognize me either time. This diary mentions working with Trish.... This can't be mine.

Again I watch as night evolves into day. Again Danny ships me off to Dr. Bandos and again I'm left there, sitting on a coach in her office, wishing to be somewhere else.

"Lay down," Dr. Bandos says gently to me. It pains me to do what she says.

"You know, I'm really much more in the mood to just talk—"

"Leslie, hypnosis is simply a way to retrieve some answers, answers to questions that maybe you yourself are trying to solve—"

"Les. My name is Les.… This hypnosis thing isn't going to work because I don't want you in my head—"

"Are you innocent?"

"What? Yeah, of course I am—"

"Then you should have nothing to hide."

Damn. Good move. Now if I argue with her, not only am I resisting questioning, I look like I'm trying to hide something. The next thing she says, however, is just uncalled for.

"If you don't cooperate, I can retrieve the same subconscious responses with the use of medication— something much stronger than the pills you're taking now."

Should be taking.

"There's no need to threaten me," I hiss, then close my eyes, preparing myself for the hypnosis I really, really don't want to participate in.

"It's not a threat, Leslie," the psychologist says sincerely. "I don't want to make you feel threatened or uncomfortable. I'm just making the situation clear to you. All I want to do is help you; I'm on your side."

Oh, like I've never heard that before.

She begins, telling me to relax and concentrate on my breathing. I'm at odds with myself in my mind. I don't want to do this, but maybe she's right. Maybe this can help me…or make me seem even crazier and more out of touch with reality than I really am.

"…And when I reach ten you will be in a state of complete peace and hypnosis…1…2.…"

No. I won't let her in.

"3...4...."

Yes, I will. I have to do this.... I'm a horrible liar, there's no way I can fake being in a state of hypnosis.

"5...6...."

I *am* innocent. This won't matter; in fact, it can only help.

"7...8...."

I'm falling, dropping into some deep inner self, a state of vulnerability...a place of peace and relief, but still vulnerability.

"9...10."

I'm in nothingness. She tells me to breathe deeply. I obey. She tells me to drop my shoulders, my head, relax my neck and back. I do.

"I'm going to ask you some questions and I want you to answer me truthfully."

Whatever you want...I have nothing to hide.

"Have you been taking your medication?"

I smile.

"No."

She sighs, disappointed with me. "All right, well keep concentrated on your breathing. I want you to think about the crime scene—the non-existing woman's bedroom. Is anyone in the house?"

REWIND. Flashing images flip past like a flip book before me. Time moves past the diary, past the theatre, back farther and farther and FREEZE."

"Jimmy and me."

"Is that all?"

Play. The scene unfolds. I watch it like I'm a fly on the wall. I'm looking around the room, Jimmy leaves, I'm attacked by the cat under the bed…. The events unfold until Jimmy and I dash out of the room. Cut to a still image of Jimmy looking at me, the card and gun in my hands, the house ablaze before us.

"No one else…except the poor cat."

"The gun you had with you…. Is that Jimmy's?"

"No."

"Is it yours?"

"No."

"Whose is it?"

"It was thrown away…Jimmy found it in a garbage bin outside the theatre in town."

"Was it loaded when Jimmy found it?"

"No."

"Jimmy told you all of this?"

"Yes."

"Do you believe Jimmy?"

Interesting question. Jimmy stands before me now, smiling innocently, his hands stuffed in his pockets. *Should* I believe Jimmy was a better question, one I'd love to know the answer to. I don't know how to answer, so unconsciously I change the subject.

"I can read minds."

Well, congrats, now I sound really crazy. Of all the things I could have said, why was this thought the one my mind spit out?

"Really? Tell me about that."

"I can read colors and numbers and cards. The non-existing woman is the Queen of Diamonds, Jimmy is sixteen and red, Molly's number is 208, my lawyer is orange, Derek is forty-two, the cops are blue—"

"Why do you do that? Label people by colors and numbers?"

A deep breath in, a deep breath out. The words spill out before I think them.

"Names cause complications. Names can be similar and deceiving. They can be made up. They can be common. Faces are easier to match with thoughts because nobody thinks the same. Thoughts can't lie or hide. Just like *you* can't hide that you actually want me to be innocent, that you feel I'm harmless, and that you're thinking you should really be concentrating on what I'm saying, but the thought that your MasterCard has just been cancelled on you keeps popping up in your head."

Silence. *What did I just do? I read her mind...* really *read her mind. How did I do that?*

"I...I thought you said you could only read numbers, colors, and stuff?" my psychologist says slowly. She sounds shocked.

"That's correct," I answer.

Credit card. Why is that important? My mind is racing faster then my mouth again.

"Credit card," it says, but I'm already lost in my memories, racing backwards in time, past the talk with my parents, past the meeting with the judge, past my arrest. Credit card was important, why was it important? WHITE. A phone rings. I'm talking to Molly on my cell. I ask her about the vacation ticket to Hawaii.

"Shit. You know what, my credit card was stolen a few days ago, I forgot to cancel it! Shit, thanks for reminding me—" PAUSE. Fast forward. I'm in the theatre, the curtains open; I'm in the past again.

"I'm in her room."

"Whose room? What are you looking for?"

"The non-existing woman's room."

I'm standing in the center of the room, looking around again. Scott was pointing things out to me... the black clothes, the bed, the smoking cigarette, the credit card—

The credit card she didn't grab before fleeing from the explosive house. She didn't grab it because it wasn't important to her, because it wasn't hers....

"It was my sister's."

"What was your sister's? What are you talking about, Leslie?"

"Credit card. She stole my sister's credit card."

"Leslie—"

"Some two queens flipped."

"Leslie, I don't understand what you're saying..." My psychologist's voice is but a whisper to me. My mind is spinning, cluttered with memories and riddles and thought. What does that mean? It means the non-existing woman exists. Does she have something to do with Dr. Patricia? Does she know where my sister is? What does the riddle mean? The film in my head is scratched and is skipping. I can't keep concentrated on what I see, on my breath, on anything.

Dr. Bandos is holding my shoulders, trying to keep me still—I must be struggling. I don't know, I'm lost in myself. She's telling me to stay calm, concentrate on my inhale and exhale. I do. The film is slipping out of existence, making it easier to think. I have to remember this.... I have to remember what I've discovered here in this odd state of subconscious.

"When I reach one and snap my fingers, you'll wake up feeling refreshed. 10, 9, 8, 7—"

"Slow down!" I shout. My response to the countdown temporarily stuns my psychologist into silence, but she picks up the countdown again, starting from where she left off, counting slower now.

"6...5...4...3...2...."

Damn. I've already forgotten what I was supposed to remember.

"...1!" SNAP.

I wake up. It feels like I've only blinked, that only a second has passed, but somehow in that second Dr. Bandos has magically transported from her seat to my side, her hands tightly clutching my shoulders. I stare at her, puzzled. She looks embarrassed and pulls her hands away.

"What happened?" I ask, really wanting to know.

"You.... Uh," Dr. Bandos returns to her seat and straightens out her black skirt and glasses.

"You were ranting about your sister's credit card."

"I was?" That's odd. What do I care about Molly's credit?

"You also mentioned an odd riddle.... What was

it…? Sum of two queens something."

"Some two queens flipped."

"What's the importance of that riddle?"

"I don't know." I sit up. "It was in a dream of mine; I'm trying to figure out what it means. Are we done here?"

"Well, uh…I suppose. Unless you have any questions for me."

Sure, I have questions, but you wouldn't be able to give me the answers I'm looking for. I shake my head.

Judge Judy. Full House. Montel. Rosie. Mad TV. Blue's Clues. Jerry Springer. News. News. News. Weather. Spanish soap opera. Hundreds of channels and nothing to watch. I turned off the TV. Molly still hadn't come home. I still couldn't reach her cell phone, and Danny still won't believe that Molly's gone. For the first two hours alone in the apartment I had, as suggested by my siblings, exercised. I would've done it for longer if it wasn't for the apartment's small size and lack of a decent sound system. For the next hour and a half I flipped through the channels on the TV while calling Jenny over and over again, well aware she wouldn't pick up because she was at work and of course didn't have her cell phone on. I called anyway. I left five ridiculous messages on our apartment answering machine, trying to disguise my voice, and watched "Who wants to marry a midget?" on Jerry Springer before falling into complete boredom. I turned off the TV and stared at my reflection in the empty screen, lying upside down on the coach.

What the hell do I do now....? I can eat.

I slid onto the floor, crawled into the kitchen, and sat on the floor in front of the refrigerator.

"Open sesame!" I opened the fridge and was disappointed. Nothing. Literally nothing to eat...probably because while I should've been shopping for food, I was instead being taken hostage in a stick up run by Jimmy.

I slammed the fridge door closed harder than I expected, causing something to snap off the top and fall down in front of me. I picked it up. In my hand was a little electronic gadget, no bigger than a bottle cap. It looked like a headphone earpiece. *Hmm.... Weird.*

I got up and walked back into the living room, still inspecting the odd little thing. It almost looked like a piece of spy gear.... *Wait....*

I slowly lifted my head and my eyes swept the room, starting low and moving up each wall until my sight settled on the ceiling fan. Something was blinking. I dropped the gadget and jumped onto the coffee table to get a better look at the fan.

Something else, just a little bigger than the earpiece thing, was attached to the center of the fan. I ripped the object off and looked at it, finding this one was more like a computer chip with a little blinking red light. What the hell was going on? Was this real?

My search began. I swept the entire apartment top to bottom, checking every crevice and cabinet. Whatever I found I lay out on the kitchen counter until I'd searched the place twice. When I returned to the kitchen counter after I'd concluded my search, I inspected each electronic gadget, researching as many as possible on the internet on Molly's laptop.

In the end, there turned out to be four audio bugs, two video surveillances, and three unidentifiable electronics, and while I couldn't be certain, I suspected the telephone line to be tapped. I sat down on one of the stools and tugged at my hair. *What the hell was this stuff doing in Molly's apartment? And, whoever bugged this place, what were they looking for? What did they want?*

I sighed, staring at the collection of high tech mini gadgets. What was going on, and what did it have to do with my sister?

"Listen to this, listen: 'Trish wants out. I can tell. She doesn't seem to understand the deed is done, and I'm not going to let her change of heart pull me down. I don't know what to do with her, but I have to take action—she's messing up my escape plan and I'm not going to let her get in the way of me and a life of fortune and freedom.' It sounds like Trish was in on the robbery!"

"Wait, okay, so let me get this straight; you think this diary belongs to the person who robbed and murdered your childhood psychologist, and you think Trish was also involved?" Danny asks me, bending over his Quick Check deli sandwich.

"Yes, basically…Can't I just borrow $5?"

"You steal my car, you starve."

"So you think Trish also has something to do

with your sister's disappearance?" Jimmy asks. He's suddenly sitting next to me. Who knows how he managed to find us, but by now, Jimmy's inexplicable appearances were no longer out of the ordinary.

"Yes, she must. I mean, the last time I talked to Molly, she was with Trish and Trish entrusting her with something important. I think that this crime...." I point to the diary on the table, "This must be it."

"Are you sure the diary isn't Molly's?" Jimmy asks lightly. Danny drops his sandwich and glares at Jimmy.

"Molly, unlike someone at this table, isn't a criminal. Les, I'm not talking about you."

Jimmy ignores the insult and turns to me.

"Who's this Trish girl, anyway?"

"Molly's roommate. She seems like the stereotypical dumb blonde, but she might know more than she's letting on—"

"Wait, what did you say?" Danny interrupts, looking at me confused.

"She might know more—"

"Not that. You said she's a dumb blonde?"

"Well, that's the point; she might not actually be dumb—"

"I met Trish; she's not a blonde!"

Silence. Jimmy looks out of it. Danny looks confused. I'm stunned.

"What?"

"She's not a blondee, she's a brunette!"

"No.... No, I saw Trish twice in Molly's apartment, she's a natural blonde with these blazing blue eyes, tall—"

"Les, Trish has brown eyes and is shorter than Jimmy!"

"Hey, I'm not that short—"

"I didn't imagine her, Danny, don't even *suggest* it!"

"Well, whoever you saw, it wasn't Trish!"

"Bullshit." I jump out of my seat and leave the table.

"Les! Shit…Jimmy, grab the diary and the food," Danny yells behind him, getting up to run after me.

I know he's my custodian, but at the moment I hardly care. I burst out the shop's front doors and take off down the street, heading towards Molly's apartment. That's the only good thing about a small town; everything's within walking distance.

Trish is a blonde, I'll prove it. Even if it isn't the same Trish—even if she's a completely different person, I'll prove that she's real. I didn't imagine her. She's not another figment, some hallucination.… I'm not as crazy as everyone is making me out to be, and I'll prove it. I only hope she's at the apartment now.

I cover the distance between the Quick Check and Molly's apartment quicker than I expected. Finally I've reached Molly's apartment building. I'm running up the stairs, now I'm racing down the hall. I feel like a madman, jamming the spare key into the lock, clawing at the knob, trying to get the door open. Finally it swings in. I run into the apartment and feel a sense of utter disappointment to find it empty. I fall onto the coach in the living room area and just sit there, trying to catch my breath and arrange my thoughts. The blonde had

to be real.… Of course I can't be certain, but it just.…
She can't.… It wouldn't be fair if.…

"I've been imagining her. The entire time, she hasn't
been real," I say out loud to myself. The statement
makes me miserable. I hear pounding at the door and
figure it must be Danny and Jimmy.

"I need the medication," I say to myself automatically, without really believing it, then get up and unlock
the door. I pull it open slowly, sighing at the floor, then
look up and am blinded again by a head of brilliant
blonde hair. Before me stands Trish.… Or whoever I
thought Trish was.

"Oh, uh.… Hey, Les! Have you seen—"

"You're not Trish," I interrupt her, not sure what to
expect. At first she looks at me and laughs, then the
smile drops from her face completely. She sighs.

"You're right." The girl who is not Trish pulls something out of her pocket and shows it to me. It's a police
badge.

"I'm detective Colly, and I have a few questions for
you. I need you to come with me, please."

I beam at her and say happily, "Thank god you're
real."

She doesn't get it, and from the look on her face, I
can tell she's not amused.

"Mark! Hey, uh, the apartment's bugged!"

"Okay.… What do you want me to do about it?"

Interesting reaction, but it's Mark, so I wasn't too
surprised.

"I mean Molly's apartment."

"Really? Molly's apartment is bugged?"

"Yes."

"Why?"

"That's what I'm trying to figure out."

"Well, maybe she doesn't trust you being alone with her stuff."

"What? No, I don't think Molly even knows that the apartment is bugged. This stuff looks pretty professional—"

"Ask Molly."

"I can't, she's missing."

There was a silence on the other end of the phone.

"What?" Mark finally asked. It was infuriating, talking to Mark.

"She's missing! She's been gone without a word for a day now."

"So you're talking kid-on-the-back-of-the-milk-carton missing?"

"Yes."

"Have you called the police yet?"

"No, Danny told me to wait around, make sure she isn't just out or something."

"But you think she's really missing?"

"Yes."

"Shit."

"Yeah, I know…. I've been walking around the apartment in circles for a while now. I put the bugs in the freezer—"

"Hey, don't break them!"

"You think I can trace them back to whoever put

them in the apartment?"

"No, not that...I want them."

"Mark, this is serious!"

"I know, I know, just.... When was the last time you saw her?"

"Molly? Um, I spoke to her on the phone yesterday.... She was upset.... She said 'I love you'."

"What?!" It sounded like something on the other side of the phone tumbled over and broke.

"Mark? Are you there?"

"Yeah, yeah, I'm fine—"

"Where *are* you?"

"Nowhere, nothing; she said she loved you?"

"Yeah, and then she said 'Don't worry about me, everything's okay' and hung up."

"Dude, Les, that's bad."

"I know," I sighed. "Maybe I should call the police—"

"No! No, Les, the apartment is bugged, that's not a good sign."

"Do you think the police have something to do with this?"

"I don't know, maybe! What if she knew or found out that someone's been watching her? If I found out my apartment was bugged, first thing I'd do is go into hiding, try to figure things out, you know?"

"You might have something there," I said. My head was whirling, my brain shifting through memories. "Once she asked me if I was in the apartment.... She said we couldn't talk there."

"She definitely knew the place was bugged, then.

Les, don't call the police.… We don't know who she's hiding from or what connection they may have. We have to find her ourselves."

"How? We're not detectives."

"Listen, I can't talk now, but just promise me you won't call the police."

"Okay, I won't. What about Danny? He still doesn't believe that Molly's really missing."

"I'll call him—"

"He's on a date with Derek, you won't reach him."

"Damn it. I don't like that guy."

"Derek? Why, he seems nice—"

"He's fake and honestly he doesn't seem interested in Danny. But whatever, I'll call Danny later."

"Well, until then, what do I do?"

"I don't know.… Call your girlfriend. By the way, she's freakin' hot—"

"Bye, Mark."

"Hey, if things don't work out between you two, can you give me her number?"

I hung up.

I'm once again at the police station. Once again I'm in an interrogation room, and once again I'm staring blankly at my own indifferent reflection in a one-way mirror. I'm very aware of the tracking bracelet on my ankle. I decide to sit up straight, my hands neatly folded in front of me, trying to look as innocent as possible.

Danny is undoubtedly outside the room giving the police a hard time. There are no words to describe the expressions on Danny and Jimmy's faces as detective

Colly and I descended the stairs of the apartment. I only smiled at them and mouthed "I told you I'm not crazy."

Detective Colly is probably behind the mirror, talking with her superiors. Finally she and another officer enter, carrying a folder of papers. Colly sits in front of me while the other officer leans over me menacingly.

"As you know, I'm Detective Colly. This," she nods to the other officer, "Is my partner, Detective Emerson."

Emerson is this big scary guy; black, bald, and tall, with exploding muscles. He wears a straight, poker face expression and towers over me like some stone castle. I look back at Detective Colly, my eyebrows raised.

"We have a few questions to ask you. First," she takes a picture out of the folder and lays it down in front of me. "Do you recognize this person?"

Before me lies a picture of Dr. Patricia.

"Um…yeah," I stutter, picking up the picture. "Dr. Patricia; she used to be my psychologist. My parents told me she was just murd—" *Wait. Why is she showing me this picture?* If she's an undercover cop, and she's been snooping around the apartment.…

"You bugged Molly's apartment. You think.… You think Molly or I have something to do with the murder?"

Colly's expression doesn't change but Emerson smiles. I'm shocked and I don't try to hide it.

"Do I need my lawyer?"

"We're just talking here, Leslie," Detective Colly

answers calmly. I interrupt her.

"I didn't—and wouldn't—hurt anyone. Why would I ever even *want* to hurt my childhood psychiatrist?"

"That's what we're trying to find out. We know Dr. Patricia let in her attackers, that there were at least two people involved in the heist, and that what was meant to be an easy robbery turned into a homicide. Have you ever been inside her house before?"

"Yeah, but—"

"Then you knew she was wealthy?"

"No, I—"

"You didn't know she was rich?"

"I was, like, ten when I attended sessions with her; I just thought she had a cool house. Anyway, until two weeks ago I was in New York City! I have my girlfriend, friends, even coworkers who can attest to that. In fact, I can call some of them up right now—"

"So you're saying you have nothing to do with the robbery?"

"Yes, I have nothing to do with the robbery. I'll take a lie detector test if you want."

"What about your sister?"

"What about her?"

"She recently went missing. Do you have any idea what happened to her, where she went?"

I try to calm myself down and think. That I'm nervous and high-strung at all is a bad sign, even if my sister and I are being accused of murder.

"No, I don't know what happened to her, but that's what I've been trying to find out. Anyway, Molly couldn't hurt anyone, let alone murder a woman she never even met."

"Then what about your missing file?" Emerson speaks for the first time. His deep voice startles me and I look up at his accusing scowl.

"What?"

"There are patient files missing from Dr. Patricia's office.... All of the 'A' files, actually. That would include your file, wouldn't it?"

"How should I know? Dr. Patricia wasn't my regular psychologist; she might not have any files for me at all. I had sessions with her for maybe two weeks while she was covering for my usual doctor, Dr. Massy. Anyway, there are a lot of last names that start with the letter 'A'—"

"Yes, but 'Adams' was the name of the patient she was supposed to meet the evening she was killed."

"…What?"

"The patient schedule in her computer had the name 'Adams' typed in for an 8 o'clock session. She was killed about that time that same night."

I'm speechless. I'm not sure what to make out of this or what to say, but now Detective Colly and Emerson are staring at me, expectantly.

"Well…I don't what to tell you. Maybe someone's setting me up, but I have plenty of witnesses to attest that I was in New York City when she was killed—"

"Can you tell us why, exactly, you were attending sessions with Dr. Patricia? Do you have a mental illness, or were you just a 'disturbed' little kid?"

I purse my lips together. I can tell she already knows the answer to that question, and despite the fact that I did take medication this morning, I can feel my hot anger rising alarmingly high.

"I'm not saying you did anything, Leslie. It just seems awfully coincidental that only a few days after you show up here, you happen to be found at the scene of some mysterious explosion—"

"I want my lawyer." *Shit, I sound guilty as hell.*

Emerson is smiling again. Colly nods, taking the picture from me and putting it back in the folder.

"That's not necessary. We're not holding you as a suspect—not yet, anyway. You're free to leave." She smiles at me. I grind me teeth and rise from the table. She waits until I'm at the door before saying, "Honestly, I don't think you did it."

I stop at the door and debate whether or not I really want to stay to hear what she has to say. She continues.

"I don't think you were at the house at all.… I think you had your siblings commit the crime for you—"

"This is ridiculous."

"We'll find those diamonds, Les."

I freeze up, remembering my dream.

"Wait.… Diamonds?" I turn around. Detective Colly is watching me closely, trying to read my reaction.

"Dr. Patricia had quite an impressive collection of jewelry. It was the most valuable of the items stolen from her house."

The Queen of Diamonds. My cell phone rings. The sound makes me jolt. Emerson and Colly look surprised as well, obviously not expecting the unpleasant interruption. Woken from my trance, I quickly leave the room. I don't pick up the phone until I'm walking out of the building.

"Hello Les," the non-existing woman greets me over the phone.

"What the *hell* is going on?!" I scream back. The non-existing woman ignores my question and asks me intensely, "Did you try to kill me a few nights ago?"

"*What?*"

"The explosion at my place; did you plant those explosives?"

"Hey, I barely got out of that house alive; if anything, it's you who's trying to kill me!"

"Shit."

"Where's Molly?"

"She's safe; shit."

"I asked you a *question*, where the hell is she?"

"You have to help me, Les."

"What? Screw you—"

"Someone's trying to kill me, the same person who's trying to frame you."

I knew I wasn't that crazy. Thank god. "…I'm listening."

"I don't want to say too much over the phone. I want to meet you in person—"

"Last time that happened, I almost got blown up."

"We'll meet at Molly's apartment—"

"Bad idea, the police bugged the place. I found most of them, but there might be…. Wait, how do you know where Molly's apartment is?"

The silence tells me all I need to know.

"*You're* Trish...." I breathe the name into the phone. *Silence*. I wait for her response.

"Yes."

The non-existing woman has a name at long last. Danny bursts out of the police station in a huff and joins me in the fresh air. From the frustrated expression on his face I can tell they must have questioned him, too. I sigh and turn my attention back to the phone.

"Where else can we meet?"

"How about the Italian restaurant next to the theatre? Tonight, okay? We'll make it an eight o'clock date." She doesn't wait for me to respond. The line goes dead and I stuff the phone back into my pocket.

"Where's Jimmy?" I ask Danny.

"He's still in questioning. Les, did you know your old psychologist was killed? Worse yet, they think—"

"—That you and I are in on it. Yeah, I know. They think Molly might have something to do with it, too— they know she's missing."

"Shit."

"Don't worry, they're not going to find her."

"How can you be so sure?"

"Because they don't suspect Trish, and she's the only one who knows where Molly is."

"What's Trish have to do with anything?"

"You know how I kept telling you about the non-existing woman? The Queen of Diamonds?"

Danny's expression is blank. Then the realization

washes over him.

"You were right, Danny. The non-existing woman isn't an actress; at least, not one in the play. Trish knows where Molly is. She says she needs help—someone's trying to kill her."

"Shit."

"Don't feel bad for her; we don't know if she can be trusted. She might be the one framing us or trying to kill us—I have no idea. She might've killed Dr. Patricia, for all we know."

Danny looks a little confused, but at this point I suppose it doesn't matter. The less he understands, the better; he's just going to get in the way. I need to talk to Jimmy...I need protection for tonight, and maybe Jimmy can get his hands on another gun. Tonight I'm not taking any chances.

Then again, if Jimmy doesn't have a gun, I guess I can always call Mark.

Mark has always been a daredevil. When we were kids, he wanted to be a stuntman. In fact, I'm pretty sure Mark still wants to be a stuntman. His dangerous hobbies started with dirt biking and has since evolved to sky diving and drag racing.

Of his dangerous activities, hunting and target practice were two that really stood out. Mom has always been terrified of guns, and here's Mark, collecting artillery as if in preparation for Armageddon. I'm sure he still has his guns hidden somewhere, and he owes me one for telling Mom and Dad about my getting arrested. In fact, I even know which one I want....

"You wait here. I'm just going to run in and tell Mark something," I tell Danny as I get out of the car parked in front of our parents' house.

"We drove all the way here just so you can tell Mark something?"

No.

"Yeah, well, I don't want to risk calling him when his phone might be tapped," I tell Danny before running into the house.

Mark lives in the small "apartment" above our parents' garage, so at least according to his standards, he doesn't actually live with our parents (unless, of course, he needs to use a bathroom or the kitchen). I run up the stairs in the garage. Mark opens the door just as I reach the top step.

"Where's Danny?" he asks, looking behind me.

"Don't worry, he's in the car."

"Good." Mark grabs my shirt and pulls me in, slamming the door closed behind us. I take a seat on the clothes-covered coach while Mark goes off to find the gun I told him I needed over the phone.

"You know how dangerous it is for you to be here?" Mark reprimands me.

"Did the police bug the place?"

"No, but they stopped by and questioned Mom, Dad, and me. Now they know Molly's missing. You're lucky the two of them just left to fill out a missing person's report, as if that would help the situation."

"They're wasting their time."

"Well right now, that's a good thing." Mark returns

with the revolver. He puts it down on the table in front of me. The two of us stare at it for a while in silence.

"Is it loaded?" I unwillingly ask.

"Yeah."

More silence. My brother looks like he wants to ask me something. Quietly he finally says, "You aren't going to shoot anyone, right?"

"What? No! Of course not...I just...I have no idea what I'm doing," I sigh. Mark sits beside me on the coach.

"Everything'll be fine. I trust you with Molly's life over anyone else in our family," Mark tells me.

"Wow, lay on the pressure, why don't you? You make it sound like if I do something wrong, I kill her."

"Don't worry so much. We're going to get her back, safe and sound."

He pats me on the back. I take a deep breath in, let it out. Finally, I pick up the gun. A chill rushes through me the moment I touch its cold handle. Simply holding the loaded weapon makes everything so much more real and dangerous. Then I hear a voice and look up. Standing in front of me is Scott.... *Great.*

"Ask Mark about the riddle," Scott demands. Even though I hate that he's here, I obey.

"Mark, I had a dream.... There was a riddle in it, maybe you can help me figure it out?"

"Sure, fire away! I'm good at riddles; did a ton when I worked at that Chinese Buffet writing fortunes for fortune cookies."

"Well it's not so much a riddle. 'Some two queens

flipped'—a Queen as in the playing card."

"…That's it? What kind of riddle is that?"

"I don't know. You know I suck at riddles."

"Okay, well, 'some two Queens' or 'sum of two Queens'? Is the answer supposed to be a number?" Mark asks me.

"What?"

"You said to think of cards. If the answer's a number, the sum of two queens is twenty-four—because a Queen is twelve in the deck, you know? Unless we're talking blackjack, then it's twenty. I don't get that flipped bit, though.…"

Scott pulls a card out of thin air and holds it out to me. There's a number burned in the center in an elegant script, more decorated and vivid than any time before.

"Forty-two," I whisper. Scott smiles a bright, secretive grin and nods.

"Forty-two's the answer? What does 'forty-two' mean?" Mark asks me.

"It's a person." I smile and look up at him, just now starting to understand. "I think I know who was behind the robbery at Dr. Patricia's."

Brendan had a notebook. I saw it. *Did it look like the diary?* I can't remember. A new memory of a talk I had with him seems to be clearing up in my mind now, like a fog starting to lift. I can't fit it in any specific period of time.… My timeline and sense of order of events is skewed. The film in my mind is scratched and tearing due to constant viewing and rewinding.

I can't remember where our conversation took place and can only assume we were at the theatre.

"Is acting what you want to do for a living?"

"Nah. This is temporary.... Maybe I'll act on the side, but I have a different source of income."

I stared at him for a moment, then realized what was missing.

"No *42nd Street* today?"

"Huh?"

"You're usually wearing some *42nd Street* clothing."

"Well, I've got a *42nd Street* button in my car."

I laugh.

"So, did you catch up with that girl?" he asks me.

"What girl?"

"The one you were asking me about. Black hair, goth—"

"Oh, yeah, I found her."

"What did you want to talk to her about, anyway?"

"I was just going to ask if she'd seen Molly."

"Molly's gone? I mean, you can't find her?" Brendan seemed nervous. I couldn't understand why. He covered up his nervousness by changing the subject.

"It's been rainy, hasn't it?"

I nodded slowly.

"I don't live too far from here," he continued. "Still a pain to walk in the rain, though...."

"...We're in Danny's car, just outside the restaurant, right now. We're waiting until we see her walk in, then I'll join her while Danny and Jimmy grab a table nearby," I tell Jenny over the phone. I can imagine her on the edge of her seat, clinging to the phone like it's a grenade.

"Well, what about the gun?" she asks intensely. I glance at Danny sitting in the front. I know he can't hear the conversation, but it still seems risky to talk about the gun while sitting in the same car.

"I'm going to have it tucked in my jeans," I whisper. "I plan to—"

"You're wearing jeans?"

"W-what?"

"You're wearing jeans to a fancy date at an Italian restaurant? Yeah, you're not going to stand out at all."

"Hey, first of all, it's not a date. Second of all, I didn't exactly pack any formal wear—"

"You packed those black pants."

"They're dance pants! They're more like pajamas, that's not formal—it doesn't matter! Focus, all right? I plan to kind of flash her the gun as I sit down, without Danny seeing."

"Why?"

"What do you mean 'why'? So she knows I'm serious and that she shouldn't try anything…If she helped kill Dr. Patricia she might be dangerous."

"What if she screams? After all, she did think you tried to kill her, now you'll be showing up with a gun."

"She won't scream. She's not the type, and I don't think she wants to risk making a scene. She just wants to talk to me…that's why she chose a public place."

"Yet you're bringing a gun."

"Just in case. Yes."

There's a moment of silence and I know what Jenny's thinking.

"I'll be fine, Jenny."

"You better be. I'll be pissed at you if manage to get shot somehow."

I laugh.

"I'll be careful."

"This is so crazy," Jenny says nervously.

"There she is!" Danny whispers, pointing out the window. The three of us watch the shadowy figure in a black, billowing dress swoop down the sidewalk and into the restaurant, stopping in the doorway to look around.

"Okay…Jenny, I gotta go."

"Wait, just one more thing!"

"Yeah?"

"Get rid of the diary."

"What?"

"Burn it. Read through it, gather all the clues, then burn it."

"Why would I do that? That's the only evidence I have proving Brendan killed Dr. Patricia—"

"But it has your name on it, your fingerprints all over the pages, and the writing sounds enough like you that if you were to show it to the cops, they might just use it against you. That diary is only going to hurt you, get rid of it. I'm sure it's just another prop planted to set you up."

I sit silently for a moment, unsure what to say. I hadn't even considered that the diary could be a fake.

It made sense, and Jenny could be right about it being part of a set-up. But the entries felt real, and how I found the diary open face-down on the floor.... It just didn't seem like it was planted there.

I hang up with Jenny.

Danny, Jimmy, and I enter the restaurant and approach the unimpressed host, disgusted with our casual garb.

"You two...Leslie and Danny?" he asks, looking down his long nose at us. We must look baffled because he immediately answers our curiosity with "Your date for the evening informed me you two would probably be dressed...."

He looks us up and down again. "Casually," he hisses.

"Yes, well—"

"Who is this?" The man's now glaring at Jimmy in dirt coated sneakers, ripped jeans, a stained sports T-shirt, and a backwards baseball cap. Jimmy opens his mouth to talk but the man interrupts.

"Out."

"Hey, now—"

"OUT!"

"Jimmy, it's okay," I say quietly. "We'll meet up with you later?"

Jimmy looks bewildered, groans, then stomps out. The host sighs and grabs two menus. Danny and I begin to follow his lead, but the man stops Danny.

"The lady was very specific in her request. You," he looks at me, "will be dining with her. You," he looks at

Danny. "You won't. Stay."

Danny looks rather shocked but does as he's told. I wave at him before being led to the back of the restaurant.

"Ah, Les," the sultry voice finds me before I spot her. "Take a seat."

She's smiling her amused little grin. Her eyes stay glued to me as the host drops the menus on the table with a thud and marches away.

As I pull up my chair, I lift up my shirt slightly, revealing the gun. I watch her eyes flicker from it back up at me. I sit. Her smile grows broader.

"Well, well. Are you implying I'm dangerous to be around?"

"Can't take any chances."

"I'm not your enemy."

"I don't know that."

She sighs. The smile fades slightly. "Your sister is safe."

"All right; tell me where she is."

Trish sighs again, unwilling to tell me. Finally she gives in.

"She's taking a much-needed vacation to Hawaii."

"She didn't buy that ticket. Her card was stolen."

"Yes, I stole it. Yet, I'm not in Hawaii right now, am I? If I had it my way—and didn't have a conscience—I'd be shooting the tropical breeze. That ticket was meant for me, but Molly caught on. Plus, your sister is just charming, I love her. She talks about you constantly; you know she adores you?"

"You killed Dr. Patricia."

I shouldn't have said that. That was a big accusation; she might not even be involved, and now I just—

"I didn't, Brendan did."

Scratch that.

"I don't know how you or Molly possibly found out—"

"Molly knows?"

Trish nods. "She understands the situation better than you do. Ah...."

The waiter has arrived. He introduces himself and Trish grabs up her menu. Her smile reappears.

"Well, the penne with vodka sauce with a glass of red wine sounds simply divine. Oh, Les, you should look for something! Could you give us a few more minutes?"

The waiter kind of bows and walks away. I'm about to say something but Trish's hand shoots forward and covers my mouth.

"Choose something to eat, then business."

"But—"

"Mmmh! No!"

My eyes narrow and I slowly lift up the menu. *This place is expensive.* I'm looking for a little while before Trish says, "Order what you want; your sister's paying!"

Trish drops a fold of money on the table. I open my mouth again but am interrupted, this time by the waiter.

"Are you ready to order?"

"Yes, I believe so!" Trish says overenthusiastically, bouncing in her seat. It's obvious that neither of us are very used to fine dining.

"I'll take the penne in vodka sauce with shrimp. Extra shrimp. And a small side salad, some bread, and oh, a bottle of red wine! I know nothing about wine, so just choose one, surprise me—"

"Hey, you want to order something…. I don't know, more affordable?" I hiss at her.

"What are you going to do, shoot me? Besides, it's your sister's money, not yours. Let her worry about it."

"And you sir?" the waiter looks at me.

Trish speaks before I have a chance. "He'll have the same."

"Very good, Madam. I'll be right back with your drinks."

Trish and I silently watch the waiter leave. I turn to her.

"You're a thief and you're a murderer—"

"I'm broke and I'm in danger. I wouldn't have ever agreed to rob the place if I knew Brendan was going to kill someone—Thank you!" The waiter's back. He sets down some waters, smiles oddly at us, and rushes away. We watch him leave silently. I turn to her again.

"What does any of this have to do with my family?"

"Well, things didn't exactly go as planned. Like I said, I didn't know Brendan was going to kill anyone, then he stole some files and I was freakin' out and…. Everything went so quickly, we just ran out of there and realized that he forgot to erase the entry from the schedule on her computer—he had arranged some therapy session with her as a pretense. Anyway, we'd already left; it was too late to go back and search the place for her computer. It's only a matter of time before the police find it."

They already have, I think. Trish continues.

"So we're taking off, we can hear the sirens, and I'm asking Brendan why the hell he grabbed those files, and he says— Ooh, that was quick!"

"The salads," the waiter says, setting one down in front of each of us. This time I don't pay attention to him and just ask, annoyed, "What does any of this have to do with me and Molly?"

"We needed a fall guy. Or girl. Person—"

"Why *us*?"

"Your name."

There's a moment. Trish starts to eat her salad while I put things together.

"Brendan's last name is Adams, isn't it?"

"Yep," Trish answers, her mouth full. "We know the doctor kept appointment schedules on her computer. Figured she probably wrote in 'Adams', and lucky for us, Brendan had grabbed you and your brother's file along with his. Then we looked you two up...You know you're on a Google search?"

"Whoa, whoa, wait...my brother?"

She stuffs more salad in her mouth, then continues. "Danny. According to his file he had some anxiety issues when he was little? Something like that—only met with the doctor once or twice. Anyway, Google told us that Danny works at the local theatre. Brendan joined the production, Danny introduced us to Molly—

are you going to eat anything?"

"I didn't know Danny had anxiety issues."

"Seriously, this salad is actually super tasty," Trish says muffled, her mouth completely full. "So the paper writes this big article about the robbery, and Brendan says we have to cover our asses. Told me to room with Molly to get access to her place—you know, to hide evidence and stuff eventually. He already stuck around Danny long enough to realize he couldn't possibly pass as a murder suspect."

"So you chose Molly?"

"Brendan thought we could make that work better than Danny."

"And she caught on?"

"Not entire-*gah*," Trish stops, choking on a tomato. She finally gets it down, gasps, and pushes her plate away from her.

"Things weren't looking too good. The papers kept writing about the investigation...I was freaked out because Brendan had gone all crazy on me...I bought the ticket to Hawaii, but then...your sister was nice to me. I don't know; we really hit it off, and I don't have a lot of girlfriends. I started feeling like crap spying on her and planning to ruin her life, and eventually I just told her everything, even gave her the ticket to Hawaii. It could've worked out, but Brendan found out Molly was missing before I could disappear, too. He also found out about your visit. He read in your file that you're a scitzo, so you became the perfect scapegoat. Oooh! Pasta!"

The waiter places the pastas in front of us. At this point I've lost all hope of getting a word in edgewise. Trish immediately starts to dig into her plate.

"Would you like the wine now or—"

"Yes, sure, just leave it on the table!" I snap. The waiter doesn't seem to notice my rudeness—or chooses not to. He puts the bottle down, sort of bows again, then leaves, nose in the air.

"And?!" I ask Trish. She looks up at me rather surprised.

"And that's it. Now Brendan knows I've been helping you guys and he's trying to kill me. You really should eat, its *soo* good!"

I try to ask a few more questions to clarify things, but Trish refuses to go any further until I eat. I look at my pasta. The heat of the dish warms my face and the light scent of fresh basil floats up to me. My stomach groans. *I might as well...*

I eat for a little while and try to collect my thoughts. Molly's safe...More than safe, she's chillin' in Hawaii. *Thank god for that.* But there's still one thing unaccounted for. I place the fork down and ask quietly, "What about the diamonds?"

Trish inspects my plate, making sure I've eaten something, then answers.

"I don't know where he hid them. The collection's worth a ton, and it looks like Brendan's gotten greedy. You help me out of this mess and help me find the diamonds, I'll split it with you—"

"Now *you're* trying to frame me. The police find me

with any diamonds and I'm screwed—"

"Then I'll sell them off. Once I find some buyers, I'll give you half the profits. I care about living more than I care about money…slightly.…" She grabs the bottle and starts to unscrew the cork.

"So, what do I do?" I ask eagerly. So far I still don't see how I'm supposed to prove my siblings and I are innocent.

"I don't know. You'll have to be creative. Now," she pops off the cork and fills my glass. "How about we enjoy ourselves?"

"I still have a million questions—"

"You get one."

Shit. Now I can't think of any. I blurt out the first thing I can think of.

"What about the photos of me, the ones in your room? What were they for?"

Trish just smiles. She fills up her glass and raises it. "To us, our survival, and our—or at least, your good health."

I look at my glass. I've never been one to turn down a drink. I sigh and toast.

"So what'd she say? Where's Molly? Is she okay? What's going on?" Danny bombards me with questions later that night when we catch up with each other again.

We're in the theatre. Jimmy's playing around with some props. Danny's grabbing everything he picks up out of his hands and putting it back in its original place. I'm dancing around the stage. I'd prefer some music, but Danny refuses, busy trying to interrogate me and prevent Jimmy from braking anything at the same time.

"Brendan is the guilty party. He murdered Dr. Patricia and is trying to frame me for it, using my schizophrenia and our last name to his advantage," I explain to Danny as I start doing pirouettes center-stage.

"What does our last name have to do with anything?"

"There's only one thing connecting him to the murder; his last name appears on Dr. Patricia's patient schedule in her computer. His last name, of course, is Adams."

"Of course," Danny groans.

"He has both our files. He used them to help track us down, might still plant them somewhere to set us up."

"*Our* files?" Danny asks.

"Yeah, yours and mine." I stop spinning for a moment to look at him. He avoids my gaze. Jimmy breaks the silence with "Sucks to be you two." My brother glares at him. I continue my routine.

"So we need to prove that we're innocent and he's guilty? How are we supposed to do that?"

"No clue."

"You're going to tell all this to your new psychologist, right? What's her name, Doctor...?"

"Dr. Bandos. Yeah, might as well tell my lawyer, too. At this point the more people that know, the better. I'm already in hot water for keeping quiet about Molly's disappearance."

"Molly's in Hawaii, right? Why not just fly her back here as a witness! She can vouch for you," Jimmy offers.

"That's a great idea. Too bad the police think she's in on it," Danny snaps.

"Well, as long as you all have witnesses to support your alibis, you should be fine, right?" Jimmy suggests.

Danny rolls his eyes. "Anyone can get friends to lie about—"

"We need to find the diamonds." I interrupt.

"Come again?"

"We need to find those diamonds. Then we can use them against Brendan."

"How?"

"Use them as leverage."

"Again, how?" Danny asks, annoyed. "You can't bring the diamonds to the police because they'd just use them as evidence against you in court, and he'll know that. He went through all this trouble to find a scapegoat; he's not just going to take the diamonds and leave us alone."

"That's not what I'm thinking. Okay, right now, he has more evidence pointing to us. What we need to do is get the police to catch him red-handed, with the diamonds and the stolen patient files. Then we have Molly and Trish and our parents and whoever else to back up our story."

"So what, we break into his apartment and search the place?"

"No; Trish told me she already looked there once

when she knew he was out. She said he's gone completely mental and paranoid, so he'll hide it in the last place anyone would think of looking."

"Wonderful, that makes things a lot easier," Danny groans.

"Trish said the one time she asked him where he stashed them, he smiled and told her it was all packed up and ready to go."

The door for the backstage office slams shut with a loud BANG.

The booming sound causes my heart to skip a beat. We freeze. The three of us stare at the now closed door. Silence.

"Trish?" Danny asks quietly.

"No, I saw her drive off," Jimmy whispers.

Silence again. We wait for we don't know what. Then the door locks. We jump towards it, tearing at the doorknob which of course won't open.

"Shit! That could be Brendan— What if that's Brendan? Shit—" I interrupt Danny's panic attack to ask if there's an exit Brendan could escape through. Danny nods.

"Then that's where he's heading! Come on! Jimmy, you think you'll be okay guarding the door by yourself?"

"Well, if I'm fending for myself alone, could I at least have the gun?"

I wince at the mention of the word and, avoiding Danny's undoubtedly horrified expression, take the gun out and hand it to Jimmy.

"Les—" Danny says slowly, eyes glued to the gun.

"We'll talk about it later, now let's go! Jimmy, it's loaded—"

"Les?!"

I grab my brother and we run out the side entrance of the theatre down into the dark alley. Behind the theatre is a small parking lot sandwiched between strips of buildings with little alleys between them. Danny and I get to the center of the parking lot and come to a stop, unsure which way to go.

"I don't like this—"

"Calm down, Danny."

"Maybe he already left?"

"Shut up, Danny."

"Look around, Brendan's not here!"

A shadow. It sprints across the white bricks of the building in front of us and races down the wall, made stronger as it passes under the flood of light from a streetlamp.

"Come on!" I shout behind me, racing after the shadow.

We seem to be just behind him. Weaving down the narrow alleyways, zigzagging between buildings, I can just catch a glimpse of him before he turns each corner. Danny's falling behind, but I won't let Brendan escape—although I have no idea what to do when I catch up with him or if that's even a safe idea.

I'm beginning to have trouble breathing, but I know I'm catching up because I can hear Brendan's wheezing. Finally I turn a corner and there he is before me, only a couple of yards ahead. I charge at him, giving it all the energy I have left, the only thought in my head, *you did this to me. I will catch you.*

"Got you," I shout as I grab the back of his shirt. I fling him up against the wall and hold him there. *I did it....*

"Les?!"

"Danny, over here! I got him!"

He's not far away now. Now we'll figure things out. Now we've finally got Brendan where we want him. At this point he's too tired to run and just stares back at me angrily while trying to catch his breath.

"I got him," I say again, more to myself. *Then why doesn't this feel right?*

"What...huh...the hell, man?" Brendan gasps.

"'What the hell?'" I repeat. I laugh.

Danny rounds the corner. I look at him, still laughing, then turn on Brendan.

"I know you killed that woman. Dr. Patricia? You thought you could pin that on me? It's *over*," I yell.

"Les—"

"Danny, I got this. We know you robbed her, and we know about the stolen jewelry -"

"Les!" Danny shouts. I ignore him and just keep talking, blowing off steam by screaming at Brendan's puzzled face.

"I know everything, Brendan. And it's over now. You're going to tell us where those goddamn diamonds are, I'll make sure of that -"

"*LES!*"

"WHAT?"

"There's no one there!"

...

"What?"

Danny's freaking out. He looks close to tears. "Shit! Les, this is bad, this is very bad—"

"What are you talking about?"

I don't understand. What's going on?

"There's no one there!" He points to Brendan who looks just as confused as me. "You're not holding anyone, you're not yelling at anyone, and we haven't been chasing anyone. Brendan is not real! There's no one here!"

Silence. I look at Brendan. He looks at me. We're silent for a moment and I'm just trying to understand... Then he smiles. A smug little grin. He starts to laugh. My own figment is laughing at me.

I start to beat the crap out of him. At this point I don't care if he's real or not. My blood is hot. I'm punching something hard and yelling. Danny's shouting something at me but I don't hear him. I'm out of control, I know, but I can't seem to stop myself.

It's not fair, I keep thinking. Everything finally made sense. But now...it's just not fair.

Danny finally rips me away from the wall and gets me to sit and calm down. I feel bad; he's never had to really look out for me before now and I can tell he's not used to it. Plus no one has ever seen me this crazy before. He's telling me to breathe; just stop and breathe. I'm starting to feel a sharp pain in my right hand. Slowly everything becomes clear.

My fists are bleeding. Brendan's gone, having disappeared into thin air. My right hand is obviously broken.… A stupid move on my part. My ankle only just healed, too.

Danny's taken control of the situation. He calls an ambulance and sits with me, wrapping my hand up with his jacket. We don't talk. I can tell he's terrified with what just happened, and I can't blame him. I *am* crazy. I see things, and I just broke my hand because of it. Maybe all of this is my fault? I don't know anymore. *Shit, my hand hurts.*

We sit in silence for about ten minutes. The ambulance comes and Danny calls Jimmy to let him know where we're heading. My hand must be pretty bad because the ambulance workers are giving me some kind of meds…I hate meds.…

Things fade to black. I'm beginning to think we'll never get Molly back, even if she is just hiding out in Hawaii.

"So, tell me what happened last night."

"I got confused, that's all."

"You broke your hand. How?"

"I punched a wall. A few times."

"Why?"

"I was upset. I'm okay now."

"And the hand?"

"It'll heal. Doesn't hurt now."

"Les, is there something you want to tell me?"

I sigh. "I'm sure you've already heard about this new

mess I'm in, having to do with some robbery?"

"Why don't you tell me?"

"The police think I robbed and killed a psychiatrist I had when I was a kid. I'm being framed…I think…I don't know." I lower my head in my not broken hand and pull at my hair. I'm still a little light-headed from the meds. The hospital put me on all sorts of numbing medications and pain killers. Plus I had to take my schizophrenia medication right after the hospital released me. The doctor at the hospital said my pain-killers wouldn't interfere with the schizophrenia medication.… I think he's wrong.

"Who do you think is trying to frame you?"

"Brendan Adams.… If he exists. I thought he did, but who I thought he was turned out to be imaginary—I think he stills exists, just not the 'he' I thought he was.… That didn't make any sense, I'm sorry."

"Have you been taking your medication?"

I sigh again and nod. The psychologist grins and scribbles something down.

"I didn't kill anyone. Someone told me Brendan did and has been setting me up to take the fall for his crimes."

"But this Brendan turned out to be imaginary?"

I nod.

"Who told you Brendan was setting you—"

"Ah, I see, I know where you're going with this. Trish told me—Trish, a *real* person. You can ask Danny and Jimmy, Derek, Molly—they've all seen her. She's the non-existing woman…or existing woman…The Queen of Diamonds chick I've been talking about."

My doctor nods at me, trying to hide her shocked expression.

"The Queen of Diamonds?" she asks. I nod. "The woman whose house burned down?"

"Brendan blew up that house; I had nothing to do with it. That is, if there is a Brendan."

"You told me just now that Brendan didn't exist."

"A person named Brendan Adams, the name might or might not be real. I heard the name for the first time from Trish. Then my mind came up with an imaginary character who I thought Brendan was. My version of Brendan isn't real, but there may be a real Brendan Adams…I just need Trish to tell me who he is, who he really is. More than the name."

My doctor takes off her glasses and starts to message her eyebrows, obviously confused.… But maybe that's a good sign. When she talks, she sounds concerned, making it seem as though she believes me.

"If, hypothetically, this was all true—that these two crimes you've been involved in are related and Brendan is behind everything, trying to frame you.… Then, aren't you in danger?"

I look down at the rug, thinking. She goes on.

"This person may be mentally ill, and if he killed once.… I feel I should tell the police about this—"

"No, no, not yet!"

"Leslie, this is serious! You can get hurt—you have gotten hurt!"

"The police won't listen if I have no proof a Brendan

Adams even exists! We go to the police now, Brendan will disappear with the diamonds and the police will pin this all on me. I have Trish; she can tell me where Brendan lives, and then maybe we can find the stolen jewelry or some evidence to expose him—"

"And what if you get caught breaking and entering? Or if Brendan walks in on you searching his house, how are you supposed to get out of that...? Hypothetically?"

She believes me. I don't know how I managed to convince her. "I'll have to figure it out," I say out loud.

My cell phone rings. Dr. Bandos flinches at the sound. I apologize before picking it up.

"Trish?"

"Where is she?"

"Derek! Hey, sorry, I was expecting—"

"Where's Trish? Is she okay?"

"You know, now's not a good time." I mouth 'I'm sorry' to Dr. Bandos who sighs and scribbles some more on her notepad.

"Danny told me everything. I tried calling Trish, but she won't pick up. Les, where is she?"

"Derek, calm down—"

"She's my friend, Les!"

"Okay, okay, I know. I don't know where she is, but she's safe right now...I think. Can we talk later?"

"Fine. Find out where she is and call me."

"Okay."

"Don't forget."

"I won't. Bye."

He hangs up. I put the cell phone away, a little

stunned. It's true I haven't known Derek very long, but I've never heard him so upset. All this time, Molly had been the center of Danny's and my attention. Now Trish was in more danger than her.

"She needs to be protected," I say aloud, adding "Trish, I mean," in response to my doctor's confused expression. It's time to end this ordeal—even if that means taking a risk and handing the diary over to the police.

I'm sitting in the theatre auditorium once again, wondering what the hell I should do next. The production *Man with Bags* has really come together—they're already starting dress rehearsals. Unfortunately, this means Danny's job is suddenly much more demanding. I can hear Danny running around backstage, trying to retrieve props, equip actors with spears and suitcases, and find replacements for props that have broken or disappeared.

Derek's not on his game today, either. He's obviously more concerned about Trish than giving a good performance.... I don't blame him. I keep flipping my phone on, calling Trish's number until the answering machine turns on, then hanging up and calling again. I've already left three messages telling her to meet me at the theatre.... *Where is she?*

In the meantime I should focus on who the real Brendan could be. How should I even go about finding him?

"Look at the clues," a voice answers. I twist to look behind me, but the voice has no body.

"Why the *hell* am I having so much trouble with this?!" I wonder out loud. I took the medication just before we arrived at the theatre. It's obviously not working. That, or I was right and the pain meds are interfering with the other medication somehow.

"Look at the clues!" the imaginary voice repeats.

"Shut up, there are no clues," I whisper.

"Well, think of Brendan, the fake one."

I don't answer. I should just ignore this voice.

"Don't you ignore me!" it answers to my thoughts. "Listen, the Brendan you knew wasn't entirely fake. I'm trying to help you, so now listen and think. He said he was an actor."

"He wasn't real."

"He said he lived nearby."

"He wasn't real."

"He knew Trish and Molly, and he knows where your brother works."

"He wasn't...." Wait...that's true, Trish told me that. I think about this for a moment, then ask, "Are you saying...? Am I saying...? Do I know the real Brendan already?"

"Hey, how the hell should I know if you don't? And stop talking to yourself; people will think you're a crazy person."

"That would be an appropriate assumption."

"Les, who are you talking to?"

I flinch, then turn around to see Danny.

"Uh.... Just, talking to myself."

"You're hearing things again, aren't you?"

"The medication doesn't seem to be working."

"Obviously."

"But I think it might help us solve this Brendan issue."

"The voices?"

"And the delusions, yeah."

"I think I need to take you back to the psychologist. We'll try a different medication until we find one that works."

"Danny, I'm fine—"

"You're sporting a tracking bracelet and shattered the bones in your hand!"

"Okay, things look bad."

"Look bad? Look—"

"Danny! This suitcase is too heavy, what's the combination for the lock?" an actor screams from onstage. For a second it looks like Danny's going to scream back at her, but he catches himself and takes a deep breath. Derek rushes to the girl onstage, saving Danny the trouble.

"Listen, you gotta go talk to Derek, he's going nuts wanting to know where Trish is and if she's okay."

"Yeah, I know."

"Danny!" the actress screams again.

"I'M COMING! Jesus Christ, Les, I'm ready to kill myself. Okay," Danny runs back to the stage, yelling "I can't *fix* it because one of you *lost the code*, all right? That's what happens when you people play around with props!"

My phone rings. It's an unrecognizable number. I

pick it up.

"Hello?"

"Whadya want?"

Trish.

"God, about time you called back. You know how many times I called you?"

"I'm busy with a guy from the insurance company. Of course, they're trying to get out of paying me, which is ridiculous because why would I want to burn down my own place and almost kill myself in the process? But hey, if it's arson, apparently, they don't want to cover it! Can you believe that? I almost *died*, my house burned down—Jesus, my cat is dead, but do they care? It makes me so angry—what do you want, why are you calling me?!"

"Who's Brendan?"

"What? You mean the Queen of Diamonds, the one who blew up my house, the one framing you, that Brendan?"

"I thought *you* were the Queen of—doesn't matter. Listen, I don't know who the real Brendan is."

"What? Well, ask Molly."

"You're kidding, right? You know I haven't been able to get a hold of her since she disappeared to Hawaii—"

"Fine, ask Danny."

"He doesn't know, either."

"But.... Danny's boyfriend—"

"Derek knows who Brendan is?"

"Derek? No! I mean, yes—I can't concentrate, okay? I'm at Molly's, I'll call you back after this insurance guy leaves."

"Can you promise me that? Because I've been calling—"

"Yes, fine, promise, bye—"

"No, no, wait! Where does Brendan live?"

The line dies and she's gone. *Wow, how unhelpful.* A hand suddenly grabs my shoulder and I flinch again. I turn around to find Detective Colly and Detective Emerson leaning over me.

"What are you two doing here?"

"How's the hand?"

"Are you following me? If you have a question, then just ask and leave me alone."

"Where's Danny?" Colly asks, smiling at the fact that I'm annoyed.

"OH MY GOD, SHUT UP! IT'S NOT THAT HEAVY! Stop whining like a baby and get over it!" Danny screams from onstage, answering her question.

An hour. I'm forced to sit around at the police station and wait an hour as the police question Danny. *What the hell is taking so long?*

Finally Danny appears, loathing in his eyes.

"So...how did it go?" I ask jokingly. Danny glares at me and opens his mouth to say something when his phone rings. He growls and picks it up.

"Hello?! Oh, hey, Derek.... No, I don't think so.... Fine, calm down, I'll ask—Hey, Les, any leads as to where Trish is?"

"Oh yeah, she called. She was at Molly's, talking to some agent from the insurance company. She might still be there."

"Yeah, she's at Molly's," Danny says into the phone. "I'm glad you called; I've been having the worst— hello? Hello?"

Danny's face turns red. He violently closes the phone and turns on me. I brace myself; Danny's about to explode.

"He hung up on me…. That shit-head just hung up on me…."

"He's probably just—"

"I'm done with him! I can't take it; he's so uninterested in me, I don't even know why we were together in the first place! I can't talk to him, we never hang out, I haven't even been to his apartment—"

"Danny—"

"I NEED TO VENT!"

I shut my mouth and nod. Usually he talks to Molly about these kinds of things. Danny continues.

"You know, he never asks about me or how I'm doing. He also doesn't tell me anything about himself, like it's all some big secret or something, and ready for this? He's constantly asking about you. It's like, uh, hi, you're dating me, not my brother, but he's literally obsessed with you. Don't worry, I made it perfectly clear you aren't gay and that you have a girlfriend, but *my god*, he always wants to know where you are, what are you doing, how's your situation with the police and your schizophrenia—ok, sorry I told him about that, but I figured you wouldn't mind—"

"Holy shit."

"Hey, I said I'm sorry."

"No, not that." My mind is racing. *Could it really be? Is it really that simple?* Suddenly everything's becoming clear.

"Jimmy's color is red. Molly's number is 208. Brendan is the Queen of Diamonds.... But it's not just that. Brendan—the fake Brendan—always wore something from *42ⁿᵈ Street*."

"Les, what are you talking about?"

"Forty-two!" Sum of two queens flipped...forty-two. Derek's number.

"The *Queen* of Diamonds.... Oh, I get it—" I flip open my phone and quickly dial Trish's number. Nobody answers. I try again. "Dammit."

"Les?"

"I know who the real Brendan Adams is. Danny, we have to get to Molly's and warn Trish."

"Wha—" I grab him and we dash to the car. I just hope we aren't too late.

There was nobody at Molly's apartment. We try the theatre next. Empty. I call Trish's number over and over again and leave several messages warning her about Brendan. Now I find myself sitting alone in the empty theatre with Danny and realize I have to explain to him that his boyfriend is actually the homicidal psychopath who's been setting me up.

"Danny...."

"Yeah?"

Okay, good start, but now I'm at a loss for words. Danny senses that something's up.

"You said you know who the real Brendan is?"

"Yeah."

"Who?"

"Um.... Well, actually, turns out we know who he is...."

"Really?"

"Yeah, he, uh, he's an actor in the play," I'm stalling. Why am I stalling? Spit it out. "See, the real Brendan.... You know, you helped me figure out who it really is."

"Les, who is it?!"

"Uh.... It's...." He might hit me. Maybe I can get Mark to tell him.

"LES!"

"It's Derek."

I wait for a reaction. Nothing's happening.

"How do you know?"

Good question. I'm not sure how to answer that. *Oh, well, you see, Scott, my imaginary friend, told me that the guy represented by the number 42 was the murderer. I was also warned by the ghost of Dr. Patricia in my dream.*

"Well, Trish was trying to tell me on the phone the last time we talked. I didn't really understand until now...."

"You think he was dating me just so he could set us up for the robbery?"

"I never said that.... But yes, basically."

"And that's why he's been asking so much about you and the police?"

"Yeah—"

"And the reason he doesn't talk about himself? So I guess it makes sense that he's a good actor, since apparently he's been pretending to like me this whole time."

"Danny, please don't—"

"This bastard was planning to ruin Molly. He got you institutionalized, is framing us for a robbery, *murdered* a person, and I've been dating the son of a bitch. And just now I led him to Trish—"

"Danny, this isn't your fault! Don't blame yourself for any of this, there was no way you could've known—"

"And I gave him the code."

"You had nothing to—wait, what now?"

"I gave him the code," Danny repeats, suddenly rising and running to the prop table. I follow him and watch, confused, as he starts to rummage through the prop suitcases, throwing them around, searching for something.

"What code?" I ask cautiously.

"To the suitcase," he says airily, no longer focused on making sense. He finally stumbles across the suitcase he was looking for and eagerly grabs it from the pile. Something jingles inside. He runs the suitcase center stage and carefully places it flat in front of us, then stands and looks at me.

"Did Jimmy ever give back the gun Mark lent you?"

"Um…yeah, he gave it back to me in the hospital parking lot. Why?"

"Do you have it with you now?"

"…Yes?"

"Could I see it?"

"Uh.... Are you going to shoot someone?"

"Give it to me."

I hesitate before pulling out the gun and offering it to him. Danny grabs the revolver, cocks it, and shoots the suitcase lock. The explosive sound echoes through the theatre and I jump back, terrified.

"Danny, what the hell?!"

He ignores me and bends down to the suitcase. I give him his space, keeping my eye on the gun in his hand. He opens the suitcase, stares for a moment, then bursts out laughing.

"Les...Les, take a look at this!"

"Will you give me the gun?"

"Wha? Yeah, here, just needed to break the lock."

Danny slides me the gun and I quickly pick it up. Danny looks at me, smiling, and moves out of the way so I could see the suitcase's contents. My jaw drops. The velvety interior of the case is covered with jewelry of gold, silver, and sparkling diamonds.

I drop to my knees and gawk at the treasure. The police weren't kidding when they said Dr. Patricia had an impressive collection of jewelry. The sparkling diamond necklaces and rings send little rainbows dancing around the suitcase. Danny reaches in to pick something up but I quickly grab his arm.

"Don't. We don't want our fingerprints on this."

"Good thinking, but I was going for that." Danny points at some papers lying hidden underneath the necklaces. I use my sleeve to take the folders out and open them up.

"The missing files from Dr. Patricia's office," I say, giving Danny the folders labeled "Adams, Brendan" and "Adams, Daniel". I keep the folder yellowing with age labeled "Adams, Leslie".

Inside are copies of insurance information, filled out psychological evaluations, and papers of notes my psychiatrist had taken down, notes probably written while I was sitting there in front of her all those years ago.

I flip through the pages in the file and stop at a picture. It's a photo of ten-year-old me, sitting smiling on the coach next to Dr. Patricia.

"I remember this," I say out loud. It was taken on the last day of my sessions with her, before I went back to seeing my regular psychologist, Dr. Massy. The photo is paper clipped to a few childhood drawings I'd made, scribbled in bright crayon and labeled in sloppy, backwards letters. There's a clumsy drawing of two smiling stick figures, one with a green shirt and purple hair. "Scott" is written above his head.

My cell phone rings and I wake up back to the present. I recognize Trish's number and quickly pick it up. Trish's quivering voice gives it all away; Derek—or, rather, Brendan—is there with her.

"H-hey, Les. Um, where are you guys? Are you still at the police station?"

"Tell him we found the diamonds and his records. Call him Derek.... Don't worry, Trish, we'll get you out of this."

The line is quiet for a moment. I wait, mouthing to

Danny what's going on and what I hear. Finally another voice answers the phone.

"So you finally figured me out?" Brendan says in a clear, emotionless voice.

"Yeah. Danny helped me realize—"

"Tell him he's a piece of shit," Danny growls.

"He calls you a piece of shit, by the way."

Brendan tsks. "And I really liked him…for a second, anyway. So, down to business; I've got the girl, you've got the gold. How about a trade?"

I hesitate, look at Danny, then at the diamonds. I suppose I don't have much of a choice.

"Where?"

"How about the scene of the crime?"

"Dr. Patricia's?"

"Other crime. Let's see what's left of Trish's house. Come alone; I see or hear a cop, and Trish might have another unfortunate accident—"

"I'm bringing Danny."

"You bring Danny, she gets a bullet. Let's keep this between you and me; after all, you know how ex's can get. Ten o'clock. Bring the diamonds, my file, and my diary; Danny told me you found it in the theatre. I must admit, I wasn't too pleased to hear you guys were reading through it. You know, that stuff's private—"

"How do I know you won't just blow the place up again once I'm inside?"

"I wouldn't do that, Les. I like you too much.… Almost as much as those diamonds. Plus, I can't lose my scapegoat, now can I?"

He hangs up. I put away the phone.

"Well? What's happening?" Danny asks.

"He wants to meet and swap the suitcase for Trish."

"Okay.… When and where, and more importantly, are we actually going through with this? Shouldn't we call the police?"

"No police. He wants me to come alone."

"Because he's planning to kill you," the childhood drawing of Scott in my hands tells me. I look down at the drawing bewildered.

"But…I'm the scapegoat," I answer the drawing. The red crayon smile on the figure flips into a frown.

"He's a lunatic and a murderer. He's going to want to tie up loose ends, you've read the diary."

I know the drawing's right, but I'm not sure I have a choice. Trish is doomed if I don't show up.… Of course, he probably plans on killing her either way.

"I'm not going to let you go alone, Les. Once he gets a hold of all this shit, what's stopping him from hurting you or Trish?" Danny repeats my thoughts.

"I'm thinking, I'm thinking.…"

We need some leverage. Lucky for us, there's plenty right here in this suitcase.

"I've got an idea. Grab another suitcase; I'll take this one with me with the files inside when I meet with Brendan. You take another suitcase with the diamonds and hide them—someplace he won't find them, like in the woods or something. Make sure you don't get your fingerprints on anything, and keep your cell on—"

"So we're not giving Brendan the diamonds?"

"Well, you're right; once he gets the diamonds, there's nothing stopping him from—well, you know. Also, call Jimmy and get the diary."

"I'm not leaving you alone with that psycho—"

"You'll have to."

"Well, what's your plan!? Something's going to go wrong."

"Then I'll bring the gun. I'll give him the files and the diary, and negotiate a trade for the diamonds after Trish and I are safely out of the building. I'll figure it out.… Don't worry, I'll be fine." Easier said than done, I realize. Even I'm panicked, but at least I hide it well.

After hours of arguing and waiting, Danny drops me off a block from Trish's burned and hollowed home. I walk the block as slowly and stiffly as one on their way to meet the devil. I have no plan, no backup, and no idea what's waiting for me. I just have a goal: get Trish and get out.

I get to the house quicker than I would've liked. The withered building looks naked and broken. Caution tape is wrapped around the perimeter, but otherwise the house stands unguarded. I get a sense of déjà vu; I remember standing here before, watching as golden flames licked the wood and brick, sending smoke billowing out the shattered windows and into the night sky.

Somewhere within the house a floorboard creaks and a voice whispers—or perhaps these windy noises are just imagined, sparked by my inventive mind. Either way, I can't just stand out here waiting. Trish and Brendan are waiting for me inside.

"Why, Les! I was wondering when you were going to quit dawdling outside and join us," Brendan says when I enter. He has a gun, as I expected. Trish is sitting on the floor behind him, her hands tied around a pillar, but somehow looking quite comfortable, smoking a cigarette.

"You okay?" I ask her. She coughs, trying to respond while keeping the cigarette in her mouth.

"She's fine. Let's speed things up. Hand over the suitcase."

I hesitate. Brendan stretches out his arm and points the gun at me. "Don't make this difficult," he says with a sneer.

I sigh and hold out the suitcase. He carefully walks forward and grabs it, then retreats backward towards Trish. He puts down the suitcase on the floor, opens it, and frowns.

"Where's the diamonds?" he demands.

"The diamonds are Trish's and my ticket out of this. We walk out of here safely, I'll call Danny and you'll get your diamonds."

"You think I'm going to trust you?"

"You'll have to. It's the only way you're going to get what you want. Only Danny knows where the diamonds are hidden. Anyway, I gave you the files—"

"Minus yours?"

"Yeah, well I figured that was my private business. Speaking of which, I'll get you your diary. I just don't have it on me right now—"

"Oh, that's right! Jimmy has it, doesn't he?"

I freeze up. How does he know about Jimmy? Brendan smiles.

"Oh, Jimmy! Come on out." he calls.

Footsteps. Someone's coming down the stairs. Brendan watches, amused, as I turn pale seeing Jimmy, diary in hand, a sheepish grin on his face. Brendan walks over and grabs the diary, cackling. His cool demeanor is deteriorating. I pay no attention to him and just stare at traitorous Jimmy, trying to burn a hole in his head with my glare. Jimmy turns red and kind of sinks under my gaze.

"I'm sorry, Les, but I've known this guy a lot longer than you. Hell, I used to rob houses with this guy! He's an old friend. Plus, he promised me a slice of the profits if I helped him out.... Come on, Les. Diamonds? That collection's worth hundreds, thousands even!"

I don't respond. Of course Jimmy would betray me. He's a thief. I'd forgotten; I should've listened to Jenny's warning.

Jimmy looks like he wants to go on, but Brendan cuts him off.

"Jimmy, grab his cell phone. Unless, Les, *you* want to call up your brother and tell him to bring the diamonds?"

My silence gives him his answer. Brendan nods to Jimmy, who starts to approach me. Every step he takes sounds like thunder and shakes the house—or, at least, that's how it seems to me. My heart's pounding. The room starts to slant. The walls twist and collide, pouring into each other. Pieces of wood drip from the ceiling like splintering raindrops.

I grab out my gun and point it at Jimmy. "Not a step closer," I growl. Jimmy freezes. He looks at me and my gun, at Brendan, than back at me. Brendan barks, "Take the gun, too."

"I'll shoot," I lie.

Brendan laughs. He can see through my tough act. Jimmy still seems unsure. If he hadn't just betrayed me, I'd feel bad for him.

He looks me in the eyes, and I suddenly have a strong sense that he's trying to tell me something.... I realize I can hear him thinking. *Red, brown, sixteen, gray....* Damn, I wish I could read actual *thoughts*, I have no idea what he's trying to say. He slowly moves closer. I grip the gun tight. I don't plan to shoot him, but I won't give up the gun without a fight.

"Hurry up!" Brendan shouts.

Then Jimmy changes focus. With his eyes and a little bob of his head, he points downward. I look and see that he's pointing to my tracking bracelet. Then a whole lot of things happen at once.

Jimmy grabs my gun. I jolt and pull back, but Jimmy's managed to hit my hurt hand. Pain shoots through my arm and I yelp like a hurt puppy. Jimmy takes this to his advantage and twists the gun downward.

BANG!

...Shit.

I let go of the gun and quickly back up, petrified. Did I shoot Jimmy?

Jimmy stands in front of me. He holds my gun in his hand and is aiming it at me. He doesn't seem to be hurt, so a new question pops into my head.

Have I been shot?

I frantically examine my body, patting around to see if I'm bleeding anywhere.

"Jimmy, what the hell?" Brendan barks. Jimmy responds, but the words that I hear are jumbled. I'm still busy making sure no one's been shot. I look down and see what Jimmy was shooting at. My tracking anklet has a large dent and the little red light on it is blinking wildly.

FLASH.

Orange. "...Don't bother trying to get it off; even if you try to break it, it'll automatically send a signal straight to the police, giving them your exact location."

I look up and catch Jimmy's gaze. He flashes me a smirk and I have to stop myself from smiling back. Jimmy hasn't betrayed me after all, thank god. All we have to do now is stall for time until the police arrive.

By now, Trish has dropped her cigarette and, unable to retrieve it, seems to have decided she doesn't like being a captive anymore.

"Untie me, Brendan. Really, this is getting ridiculous."

Brendan turns on her, looking shocked.

"You think this is a joke?"

"'So there are three guys in a burned up apartment. One's a schizophrenic, one's a wanna-be gangster, and one's a gutless fruit cup....' Sounds like a joke to me—"

"All right, then, I'll let you in on the punch line; you die!" Brendan growls, cocking the gun.

"Hey, hey, let's not do anything drastic—"

Brendan cuts me off.

"Call Danny, get him to bring the diamonds—Call outside, so he won't hear anything in the background," he tells Jimmy.

Jimmy nervously glances at me before leaving the room. Brendan smiles and suddenly his demeanor is calm again. He becomes relaxed, his smile placid. He saunters towards me.

"Poor little Leslie. I really feel bad about this. It's a shame.… You and I have so much in common. We could've made a great couple."

"Okay, for the record, I have a girlfriend—sorry Trish," I add in response to Trish's disappointed expression. Brendan's smile only grows.

"But really, we're quite similar, you and I. We both like theatre, we both dream of something bigger and better.… According to doctor records and police reports, we're both insane—"

"I'm not a murderer."

"The police don't know that."

He circles me like an animal examining its prey.

"If we had the time, I would pick your brain. I'd love to know what it's like to be a schizophrenic."

My attention is seeping away from his words to the doorway behind him where Jimmy stands, trying to signal something to me.

What? I mouth when Brendan can't see. Jimmy continues to mime. It looks like he's planning to sneak up on Brendan. I don't know what he plans on doing next, but I'm sure it won't end well and try to shake my head 'no'. Jimmy ignores me and starts to approach Brendan from behind as Trish silently watches with wide eyes.

"Tell me, Les.… What brings on a schizophrenic episode?"

"Uh…stress, mainly," I shake my head some more, trying to make my movements look as natural as possible. Jimmy continues to ignore me and inches closer.

"How about now? You see anything?" Brendan asks. I glance from Jimmy back to the doorway from which he entered. Scott's leaning there, watching Jimmy and shaking his head.

"Yes," I breathe, my voice barely above a whisper.

The sound of sirens can suddenly be heard in the distance.… The police are on their way. Brendan hears the sirens, too. His expression turns dark. Jimmy has stopped for a moment to hear the sound as well. In our moment of stillness Scott leaves the doorway and stands beside me.

"Get ready," he whispers in my ear.

Brendan's staring at me. His eyes move downwards and he sees my damaged tracking anklet…he's putting it all together now.

"Here it comes," Scott whispers as Jimmy raises the gun he took from me, readying himself, planning to knock Brendan unconscious with the handle. I hold my breath. Jimmy takes one more step and....

CRACK!

The pressure was too much for the floorboards to handle. I watch, shocked, as the floor crumbles out underneath Jimmy and he plummets through the floor completely. Brendan jumps at the sound and twirls around, surprised to see a great big hole in the floor behind him.

I can hear Jimmy hit the basement floor with a thud, followed by a long moan of pain. Brendan bursts out laughing.

"You thought you could sneak up on me, you back-stabbing shit?" he yells into the hole. He points the gun down at Jimmy.

"What the hell are you standing around for? Do something!" Scott yells at me. A surge of energy rushes through me and I jump at Brendan, grabbing at the gun and pulling it upward.

BANG!

The bullet flies off into a wall. I elbow Brendan in the stomach and wrestle him to the floor, trying to grab away the gun. I've never been an excellent fighter, but I seem to be better than Brendan, and that's all I need.

"Come on, Les! KICK HIS ASS!" Trish shouts at us, struggling in her ropes.

Need the gun, must get the gun, need gun, must get it, must get it, must get it.... *GOT IT!* I manage to pry the revolver out of Brendan's hands but hardly have time to celebrate when the floor starts to crack beneath us.

"Uh oh," Trish says, trying to point to the splintering wood. I look at Scott. He shrugs.

"Shit."

CRACK! Suddenly Brendan and I are falling through nothingness, like a dream. My heart jumps into my throat. It's probably just me, but the fall seems endless, like Alice floating down the rabbit hole. Then we hit the ground.

I smash against the concrete basement floor and have the wind knocked out of me. Jimmy squeals—I landed on his leg. Brendan lands next to me. Pieces of splintered wood rain down on all three of us.

I slowly peel myself off the floor, gasping for air. Jimmy continues to moan, and Brendan's coughing, trying to get the dust out of his lungs. I sit up straight and crack my back.... *Damn. Kenneth, the director at my dance company, is gonna be pissed with how beaten up I am when I get home.*

"Hey, the police are here...! Excellent response time," Trish calls out to us.

"Jimmy...ow... You okay?"

"Oh yeah, I'm fine. You broke my freakin' leg, but I'm fine."

I get off his leg and try to stand but my ankle kills. Then I realize I've dropped the gun. I look around frantically for it and notice it lying next to Brendan.

I didn't really have a chance. Brendan grabs the gun, cocks it, and points it at me. Because we're only a few feet away from each other, he has the gun aimed at my forehead. Too close to miss.

I lose my breath again. The world freezes and there's silence. There's no Scott. No thoughts of colors or cards. My life doesn't flash before my eyes. I just see Brendan staring at me, his gun in my face, and I don't blink.

"Drop the weapon!" a voice echoes down to us, breaking the silence. Brendan and I continue to just stare at each other. Brendan keeps the gun on me.

"I said, put down the weapon!" I can hear several cops scrambling above us, but Brendan still hasn't moved.

I search Brendan's dark eyes. There's a glint of light in his pupils, just large enough to peer inside and see past the rough exterior. I dig into his mind and see someone who's disturbed. Someone who could've been different had he the parents and the help I had growing up. I see a dreamer, a screwed-up artist. I feel cold neglect and loneliness. I see silver, a playing card, the number forty-two…but there's no senseless killer hiding in these dark eyes.

"For the last time, put down the weapon or we *will* fire!" the cop shouts. Brendan blinks and I'm shut out. Then Brendan's arm loosens and he lowers the gun slightly. He smiles a dim, sad grin of defeat, and throws the gun away.

The silent moment is broken, and the cops start to bark orders at each other, orders at us: "Put your hands above your head!" and there are footsteps and creaking as officers scurry around, trying to find the stairs.

"It was never personal," Brendan says quietly to me. I nod and find I'm able to smile back.

"What happened next?"

"They arrested him. I told them everything; my lawyer thinks she can get all charges dropped.... Brendan's pleading insanity, which seems appropriate."

"What about Trish?"

The projector in my head whirls to life once more, finally fixed and functional. I pass back through the images and dialogue to that day a little less than a week ago.

The scene plays before me as vivid as if I'm witnessing it all for the first time. Trish is being escorted into a police car. She's flirting with the officer helping her in, telling her side of the story. In her story she portrays herself as Brendan's innocent captive, rather than a criminal associate.

"She'll be fine," I hear myself say.

"And Molly?" Dr. Bandos's voice quietly asks.

FLASH. Fast forward. Mark, Danny, Mom, Dad, and I are at the airport waiting. I'm flipping through a magazine, not really paying attention to what I see on the pages. Danny's pacing impatiently. Mark's hitting on the girl in the seat next to him. Mom and Dad watch the gate without blinking.

Finally the doors open. We all stand. A flood of people rush out, men and women in business outfits, families in Hawaiian T-shirts, groups of Hawaiian tourists—we're straining our necks to look over the crowd and find Molly.

Then we see her. In the vast sea of strangers there's little Molly, standing alone, clutching a small suitcase, her puppy-dog eyes desperately searching the terminal until she sees us. She beams.

"She's relieved to be home," I say, smiling myself. I hear scribbling, then Dr. Bandos takes a deep breath.

"Now, the bigger question; how do you feel about this being our last session?"

"I can't wait to go home to NYC," I say immediately. I desperately miss Jenny and Bongo—I still haven't finished telling them what happened with Brendan and all.

"I suppose you're also happy to have that thing off your leg, huh?" Dr. Bandos laughs.

I nod. More scribbling.

"Well then, I suppose we can bring this to a close. I'm going to count backwards from 10 to 1. When I reach one and snap my fingers, you'll wake up feeling refreshed."

No, duh. It's sad how this has become second nature to me. Dr. Bandos counts down and I start to feel lighter, floating back to a state of consciousness.

SNAP! I'm awake. I rub my eyes, sit up, and yawn. Dr. Bandos is smiling at me. I'm not really sure why and just smile back.

"It was very interesting working with you, Lesl—I mean, Les. When you come back to Jersey, maybe you can pay me a visit?"

I nod. "Actually, I have to stay for yet another week… as a witness in the trial, you know."

"Ah."

"But I'll stop in to say good-bye before I head back to New York."

It's hard to believe that this whole time I've just been an hour away from my comfortable city apartment. With all that's happened, it feels like New York City is light years away, an unreachable wonderland.

Dr. Bandos and I shake hands and I leave her office. I'm surprised by who's waiting for me just outside the room.

"Jenny!" I run over and grab my smiling girlfriend in a deadly, choking hug. After spinning her around a bit, I release her and wait happily for her to get air back in her lungs before I ask what she's doing here.

"You said…just a moment." Deep breath. She straightens herself and starts again. "You said in your message that you still had to go to court, being a prime witness and all, so I was thinking, 'God, that'd be interesting' and decided I had enough of waiting around for you. I figured I could help you with your testimony, you know…that and I'm tired of being left out of all the crazy adventures you've been having lately—"

"I missed you too."

I kiss her. As we leave I fill her in on the events following Brendan's arrest; returning the diamonds to the police, Jimmy's broken leg, and Danny's plans to take on Brendan's role at the community theatre. I'm telling her about Molly's return, Brendan's plea of insanity, and Trish's fictitious story of innocence when I have the most bizarre feeling of *déjà vu*—as if I'd just gone over the whole story. Strange…I can't seem to remember.

ABOUT THE AUTHOR

This is **Tracey Landau's** debut novel. Her poetry has previously been published by the American Poets Society. She currently lives in Florham Park, New Jersey. Watch for her upcoming novel from Borgo Press: *Stranger Son*.

THE *LUCKY DUCK* AFFAIR

In need of a vacation, private detective Amos True and his companion, Polly St. Jough, accept an invitation to relax aboard Otto Laird's slightly illegal gambling ship, the *Lucky Duck*. Joining them are movie starlet Clair de Lune, enthusiastic writer Ruth Booth, and a number of other suspicious characters

But True soon learns about Laird's ulterior motive for inviting him and Polly out to sea. The *Lucky Duck* has become haunted by the ghost of Captain Henry Robbins, a smuggler who years ago commanded the ship. When first one guest and then another is murdered, the ghost of Captain Robbins is the main suspect. Can Amos, with the help of Polly, uncover the real culprit? Another great off-beat mystery by the author of *Dangerous Hardboiled Magicians*!

Borgo Press Books by MEL GILDEN

Dangerous Hardboiled Magicians: A Fantasy Mystery (Cronyn
    & Justice, Book One)
The Lucky Duck *Affair: A Tale of Mystery*
The Planetoid of Amazement: A Science Fiction Novel
The Return of Captain Conquer: A Science Fiction Novel
*The Sea Was Wet as Wet Could Be: A Cronyn & Justice Fantasy
    Mystery* (ebook only)

THE *LUCKY* DUCK AFFAIR

A TALE OF MYSTERY

MEL GILDEN

THE BORGO PRESS
MMXIII

THE LUCKY DUCK AFFAIR

FIRST EDITION

Published by Wildside Press LLC

www.wildsidebooks.com

DEDICATION

For Nick and Nora Charles,
who were there first

CONTENTS

CHAPTER ONE: Chance Meeting at a Mexican
Restaurant. 9

CHAPTER TWO: Beyond the Three-Mile Limit . 19

CHAPTER THREE: Too Many Feelings 30

CHAPTER FOUR: Dancing with the Captain . . . 41

CHAPTER FIVE: Zoltan Explains. 55

CHAPTER SIX: True Takes Charge 59

CHAPTER SEVEN: The Turkish Dagger 69

CHAPTER EIGHT: Two Visitors 79

CHAPTER NINE: The Ghost Speaks 84

CHAPTER TEN: Loose Ends 93

ABOUT THE AUTHOR. 101

CHAPTER ONE
CHANCE MEETING AT A
MEXICAN RESTAURANT

Amos True looked out over the Hollywood Hills and smiled. Because it was spring, and Los Angeles had just experienced one of its rare rainstorms, the bushes and trees were a deep green. Cool air rolled in off the hills, and True hungrily inhaled the fragrance of sage and eucalyptus—they pleasantly spiced the smell of the eggs, bacon, toast, and coffee that were half-finished on the table before him.

"What are you smiling at?" the woman across the table asked. She was slim, one might say almost willowy; her pert round face under short dark hair had something of the elf in it. It would be easy to believe she was kidding or trying to pull a fast one even when she was not doing either.

"Just you, my dear Polly," True said. "You and the hills and a pretty fair breakfast. It's a beautiful morning."

"Breakfast on the patio," Polly St. Jough said with satisfaction. "How civilized. And you deserve it," she went on. "We both do after all that trouble with the two

divas."

True shuddered. "I knew there was a reason I didn't like opera."

"Opera is not the problem."

True frowned. "No," he admitted. "Murder is the problem, as usual." He carefully buttered a slice of toast while Polly sipped her coffee.

"You need a vacation," she said. "And I will help you take it. Nothing will wear a person out like dealing with the dirty little secrets of other people."

"Those dirty little secrets paid for this civilized breakfast," True reminded her.

She kicked him under the table, doing little damage to either her slipper-clad foot or his stockinged shin. True was a big man; his enemies—of which he had a few, both social and professional—often described him as looking like a gorilla. He was not handsome, exactly, but had a pleasantly ugly mug, and his brown hair was always well-barbered. People who met him for the first time were often surprised by his grace. "You know what I mean," Polly said.

True meditated while he nibbled some of his buttered toast and chewed. "Yes," he said at last. "I know exactly what you mean. But here's an idea. We'll take the Auburn up the coast and have lunch in Santa Barbara."

Her eyes got big, but Polly attempted to look innocent. "Then what?" she asked.

True said nothing, but wiggled his eyebrows at her lustfully, like Groucho Marx.

Polly laughed, sounding like a tuned set of bells.

True leaned across the table at her, about to confide more, when deep in the big white stucco house behind them the front doorbell rang out the chimes of Big Ben. True threw down his napkin and walked quickly into the house.

"If it's Lieutenant Ochoa with news of someone's dirty little secret," Polly called after him, "tell him we are full up and don't want any more."

True chuckled as he approached the front door and pulled it open. Waiting on the step was a slim man in a brown suit that was only slightly darker than the color of his skin. He had a pencil-thin mustache, beneath which was a shy smile. He held his fedora in one hand.

"Why, Lieutenant Ochoa," True cried with delight. "Polly and I were just talking about you."

"That can't be good," Ochoa said as he stepped inside the house.

"No need to be suspicious," True said. "Have you had breakfast?"

"I was hoping you would ask."

"I don't suppose you are here just for the free food," True said as he led Ochoa along the cool dim hallway to the back patio, stopping briefly in the kitchen to pick up a coffee mug.

"Of course not. I'm here to bask in Polly's warm glow."

"I thought so," True said as he and Ochoa emerged into the sunlight.

"What's that about a warm glow?" Polly asked.

Ochoa gave her a quick peck on the offered cheek, and sat down at the table. He took a piece of toast and began to slather it with butter. True filled the clean coffee mug and Ochoa took a quick sip. He sighed with pleasure.

"Well?" True asked.

"Well, nothing," Polly said. "If you're here to tell us about some new horror, we don't want to hear about it."

"No. As a matter of fact I'm here to report that something has gone right for a change. Famed opera singer Madame Von Klempt has confessed to the murder of Madame Francesca."

"You see, Amos," Polly said, "it's officially time for a vacation."

True grinned. "That's fine, fine," he said. "Are you sure that's the only reason you're here? That and to bask in Polly's warm glow?"

"Now who's suspicious?" Ochoa asked.

The police lieutenant finished his breakfast quickly and stood up while he tapped his mouth with a napkin. "Sorry to rush off," he said.

"Crime won't wait," True suggested.

"You got that right."

After True had escorted Ochoa back to the front door, he returned to the breakfast table and stood next to Polly, who was still idly sipping her coffee.

"Let's get cracking," True said as he began to collect dirty dishes. "We're burning daylight."

Just this once they left the dirty dishes in the sink. They hurried down to the garage where they got into

True's Auburn Speedster, a long bone-white automobile that, despite its length, seated only two comfortably; it was mostly engine at one end and mostly trunk at the other.

True quickly navigated the switchbacks and hairpin turns that would take them from his home down the narrow road past other stucco houses hidden behind walls and dense foliage. Like True, most of the people who lived in the hills liked their privacy and could afford to maintain it.

At Sunset Boulevard he turned right and headed west. The traffic was not bad in Hollywood that morning. Soon they passed Sid Grauman's Chinese Theater, and the spire of the optimistically named Crossroads of the World. In Beverly Hills the street suddenly became residential, and they motored past long, low, ranch-style houses with front lawns big enough to accommodate putting greens. The university came up on their left and was behind them in an instant. As Sunset became more snake-like, the houses got farther and farther apart, and soon they were driving between rows of eucalyptus trees and wide open fields dotted with cottonwoods and live oaks. At last they reached the coast route and True turned north.

The cliffs of Santa Monica rose on their right while on the left waves marched in across the sparkling ocean from Japan and hurried up onto the sand. The fresh sea smell compounded of sea salt and kelp invigorated them. Polly laughed and playfully punched True in the shoulder. They drove past beach towns, some of which

were no more than a bar and a gas station huddled together against the salt spray.

The trip to Santa Barbara was a pleasant drive of about two hours, and when they arrived True sought out Veracruz, his favorite Mexican restaurant.

"*Señor* True," cried the *patrón*, a man in a frilly white shirt and black pants.

"Javiar," True cried in response and they hugged like brothers. Javiar bowed politely to Polly, then lead the two of them toward an empty table.

"Amos True, is that you?" a large man called as he half-stood up at a table on the other side of the room. He had thin reddish-brown hair and a hang-dog face.

Javiar stopped, uncertain what to do. He looked to True for guidance.

True looked across the room and immediately smiled. "Is that you, Otto?"

"It is. Come sit with us."

True twirled his finger at the man and his table, and Javiar dutifully led him and Polly to it. True shook hands with Otto. "Polly, this is Otto Laird. We were in college together. Though I think both of us had more hair back then." He introduced Polly, and Laird said he was charmed.

Then Laird introduced the other man at the table. "This is Zoltan," he said.

"How do you do, Mr. Zoltan?" Polly said.

"Just Zoltan," the man replied using the remains of a European accent True could not identify. A tiny smile came and went quickly on Zoltan's face.

Zoltan had no hair whatsoever, and a triangular head with his chin making a single point at the bottom. His brilliant blue tie, whose color was obviously chosen to match the astonishing color of his large eyes, was decorated with astrological symbols.

Javiar brought a pitcher of margaritas as well as the usual silverware and napkins for True and Polly.

True sipped his drink and smacked his lips. "It's been a long time," he said.

Laird agreed. He seemed a little uncomfortable. "Perhaps it is fortunate that we ran into each other."

"That sounds ominous," Polly remarked.

"Yes." Laird glanced at Zoltan, who nodded in reply to Laird's unspoken question.

Before either of them had a chance to explain, a waitress in a colorful Mexican peasant outfit approached the table and took their order. Because neither True nor Polly had had a chance to look at the menu, they both had "the usual."

When the waitress had retreated, True asked the logical question: "Why is it fortunate that we ran into each other?"

Laird sighed. "As you may have heard, I recently bought an old cruise ship, which I've refitted as a luxury resort for gambling and general relaxation. I call it the *Lucky Duck*."

"I've heard about your ship," Polly said, "but I didn't know gambling was involved."

"You don't mix in the right circles," Laird said. "Word gets around."

"Gambling is illegal in California," True said. "You must be beyond the three-mile limit."

"That's right. And I've been doing pretty well out there so far. Then, about a month ago the ghost of Captain Henry Robbins began to haunt my ship."

"Who?" Polly asked.

"Captain Henry Robbins, the previous captain of the ship. It was called the *Hippocampus* back when Captain Robbins was in command."

"Assuming there are such things as ghosts," True said, "why would he haunt the *Lucky Duck*?"

"Opinions vary," Laird admitted. "Anyway, since he began, business has fallen off seventy-five percent. Most people are afraid of ghosts whether they admit it or not. I certainly am."

"Very wise," Zoltan said. "There are few things more dangerous than an angry ghost."

"You sound as if you've had experience in this area," Polly suggested.

Zoltan inclined his head once in her direction.

"That's why I hired Zoltan," Laird admitted. "He is a medium."

"Ah," True remarked.

"I know that tone," Zoltan said. "I have heard it from the mouths of unbelievers before."

"Well," True said in a placating voice, "let's say I am more inexperienced than unbelieving."

"Nicely said," Zoltan admitted.

"Nice of you to say so," True said. "But you obviously have your expert, Otto. Nothing you've said so

far explains why you feel fortunate for running into me."

"Actually, it has nothing to do with the haunting. I'd merely like to invite both of you out to the *Lucky Duck* as my guests. I'm throwing a little party for Clair de Lune and her director, Brad Windsor. You know them?"

"Not personally, but I read the papers. Miss de Lune is supposed to be the next big thing in moving pictures."

"That's her," Laird agreed. "Come on out this evening by water taxi. Gamble or not. Stay as long as you like."

True thought for a moment. "A lot of water under the bridge, Otto."

"Many gallons," Laird agreed. He stared at True as he waited for the answer, as if the answer were of more than casual interest.

"We've been needing a vacation," Polly said. "This sounds like fun."

"You heard the woman," True said. "We'll be there."

"I'm pleased that's settled," Laird said.

The rest of the meal was spent in general conversation, mostly comprised of True and Mr. Laird relating adventures they'd survived in college.

"That never happened," Polly remarked again and again. "Did that really happen?"

"Some of it," True admitted. "There was really no cow involved."

"I believe it was a dog," Laird added.

Zoltan didn't say much while all this was going on,

but he did managed to crack a smile occasionally. He ate very neatly. His own margarita seemed to have no effect on him.

After a while Mr. Laird took Zoltan away, leaving True and Polly to look out a big picture window at the parade of tourists passing by, and at the ocean crashing into the beach beyond.

Polly looked at her watch. "If you really intend to visit the *Lucky Duck* this evening, we'd better start back."

True took a sip of his drink and smacked his lips gently. At this point there wasn't much left in the glass but crushed ice. "We wouldn't want to disappoint Otto," True said.

"We could, you know."

"And we would if his invitation was just a friendly gesture."

"You think there's more to it?" Polly asked.

"I do. But I couldn't tell you why."

"One of your 'feelings'?"

"A nuisance, I know—"

"Maybe he just wants a bigger crowd for Miss de Lune's event."

"Maybe."

"*Gracias*, Javiar," True said to the *patrón*. "Superb as usual." He paid the bill and left an enormous tip.

CHAPTER TWO
BEYOND THE THREE-MILE LIMIT

Polly thought it would be too cold out on the water for her new gown, so she wore a much older and heavier silver number that she had always liked. True wore what he called his admiral suit: a double breasted blue blazer with gold buttons. In addition, each of them packed an overnight bag.

As Polly had predicted, the air was cold, and it pummeled them with light fists as it brought them far-off recorded dance music. The smell of cheap grilling meat wafted down the strand from the food stands.

"After today's lunch I didn't think I would ever be hungry again," Polly said. "But there really is nothing like the heady fragrance of hot grease."

"I'll have Otto's chef make up some for you special," True said.

Polly stuck out her tongue at him.

They walked arm in arm through the light crowd to the end of the promenade where a small power boat with a green hull bobbed gently at the far end of a short pier. A single leather seat ran around the back and

down both sides of the boat's cockpit. Sitting behind the wheel was a well-bundled man with his hands in his pockets. He had a broad face, and points of dark hair strayed out from under his flat cap.

A few miles out on the water True could see the lights of what could only have been the *Lucky Duck*. A big searchlight swept the area around it. "Is that the hell ship?" Polly asked.

"That's it. But don't let Otto hear you calling it that," True said. "He has always prided himself on running a refined operation."

"No wonder the two of you got along so well," Polly said.

When he saw he had customers, the pilot gathered himself together and stood up. "Going out to the big ship?" he asked.

"What's the fare?" True asked.

"A quarter for each of you to go out. Coming back is free."

"That sounds about right," True said.

"Somehow, I am not encouraged," Polly said as True helped her into the small boat. They huddled together in the stern as the pilot started the engine. It coughed twice, suddenly roared, then settled down to a happy chuckle.

"Hang on tight, folks. The ocean is mighty wet."

True and Polly got a good grip on each other, but except for the sociability of it they needn't have bothered. The boat putted slowly past a few rowboats and a magnificent sailboat with its sails furled, and then out

into the bay.

"First time out?" the pilot asked.

"That's right," True said.

"I thought so. Haven't seen you before. Never forget a face."

"Well, Amos has that kind of face," Polly confided.

True glanced at her, eyebrow raised.

"Yessiree, bob. I've seen 'em come and I've seen 'em go." He laughed. "They arrive with a pocket full of money and a head full of dreams and leave wearing a barrel."

"You mean they lose their shirts?" Polly suggested.

"Among other things," the pilot agreed. "Sometimes I have to loan 'em change so they can call a friend to drive 'em home."

"Say," True inquired, "does this tub ever go any faster?"

"Oh sure. We could win the derby in this thing." The small boat continued to putter along.

"I think that was a carefully veiled suggestion," Polly told the pilot.

The pilot looked back at her with a surprised expression. "Oh sure. I get 'cha. Yessiree, bob." He pushed a throttle forward and the engine roared, making the boat seem to leap into the air. True and Polly clutched each other as the boat flew along, seemingly slicing off the tops of the waves as spray spattered their faces. They would soon arrive at the *Lucky Duck*. The other advantage was that the engine was now making too much noise to allow conversation.

The lights of Santa Monica fell behind them and seemed to join together until the coast was a single bright bracelet. They broke through wisp after wisp of fog, and the lines of the *Lucky Duck* became more distinct. True had to keep revising upward how big the ship was. Many windows were lit, making the ship look like an office building lying on its side. It was held in place by hawsers as thick as a strong man's arms.

The pilot swung the boat around, throwing up a wall of water, and giving True a temporary queasy feeling before the boat bumped gently against a floating landing stage that was connected to the ship by a wide gangway. There was enough room on the stage for a hundred people or so, but at the moment there were only two. The pilot tossed a line to a man dressed like Donald Duck—plus pants—and he wrapped it around a cleat in the stage. Standing near the Donald Duck man was a slim woman with long dark hair that caught the light shining from big lamps on the deck of the *Lucky Duck*.

The pilot and the Donald Duck man helped True and Polly up onto the landing stage—which was something of a trick because they had to wait until the boat and the stage were in sync, rising and falling at the same time. When the trick had been performed, the pilot handed up their overnight bags and waved at them. "Good luck," he cried. "Don't take any wooden nickels! Keep your powder dry!" He turned off the engine and hugged himself against the cold.

"Welcome to the *Lucky Duck*," the slim woman said

gaily as she picked up a bag in each hand. "I'm Juanita Núñez, the hostess and official greeter. If I can help you with anything, please do not hesitate to ask."

True introduced himself and Polly, and immediately Miss Núñez' became serious. "Yes, of course," she said. "Mr. Kepler told me to expect you. He'll want to know you've arrived. Would you come this way, please?"

"Not expecting any more guests this evening?" Polly asked.

"Not tonight," Miss Núñez said. "You're part of a very exclusive group."

Polly raised her eyebrows at True, and he shrugged.

True and Polly had trouble maintaining their dignity as they tried to get their sea legs on the rocking platform, but it was a pleasure to watch Miss Núñez walk across the stage and up the gangway as if she'd been treading the bucking surface all her life. At last they were up the gangway and on the deck of the *Lucky Duck*, which by comparison seemed as solid as a continent.

Miss Núñez led True and Polly through a revolving door that gave the impression it was the entrance to one of Los Angeles' better hotels. Inside the illusion continued.

"Not much of a crowd tonight," True said as he looked up and down the beautifully appointed but empty hallway.

"As I said," Miss Núñez explained, "we're having a private party this evening. You two are the last to

arrive. Everyone else is in the main salon for dinner and dancing." In the brightly lit hall True could see she had olive skin and an exotic face. She was wearing a green sheath that shown with golden highlights as she moved. Altogether, she was quite lovely. "This way, please," she said and gestured for them to follow; they did so. True seemed to be fascinated by her rolling gait.

"She has a movement like a fine watch, don't you think?" Polly whispered.

"I hadn't noticed," True claimed innocently.

"Of course not," Polly agreed with a more or less straight face.

Miss Núñez showed them to adjoining rooms, leaving one bag in each room. "Call me if you need anything," she said.

"I have my tooth brush," True said, "but you never know."

"I must see to our other guests," Miss Núñez said. She smiled at him and escaped as True began to unpack. He finished and sat down on the bed to wait for Polly. When she came to the door a few minutes later, he could see that she had refurbished her makeup.

"What now?" Polly asked.

As if in answer to her question, someone knocked on the door. "Come in," True called.

A dark well-chiseled man entered. He looked like a high-ranking movie gangster; even in his tuxedo he couldn't hide his muscles. However, his smile was pleasant and he met them cordially. "I am Marv Kepler," he said, "Mr. Laird's assistant." They shook

hands all around.

"Welcome to the *Lucky Duck*," Mr. Kepler said. "I will tell Otto that you are here. He suggested you have dinner, dance if you'd like, and look around a little. No hurry."

"When we spoke earlier, I got the impression that something was bothering him," True said.

"Otto will speak to you about that. This way, please," Mr. Kepler said and made a gesture that suggested they follow him out the door. As they strolled along the hallway, music began and became louder. True recognized "The Way You Look Tonight."

Mr. Kepler led them to a large room tricked out like a nightclub. Over the door, in letters designed to look like seaweed it said Neptune's Hideaway. The décor was a mix of items that suggested both the sea and the casino: sea shells caught in nets, paintings of sailing ships at sea, leaping fish, craps layouts, roulette wheels, card spreads—the result was a little confusing, but it let the guests know what sort of experience they were in for. In a corner, three waiters watched the scene glumly. The band, whose members were dressed like sailors, was doing its best to create some excitement, but only one couple was dancing on a floor big enough for basketball. The man, with a face that was florid from exertion, was large and round and much older than his partner, who was Clair de Lune, a strikingly beautiful woman wearing a low cut gossamer gown that left no doubt that she was female and had a terrific figure.

"Will you dance with me, Amos?" Polly asked wistfully.

"I'll squire you around the floor," True said. "But I make no promises that what I'm doing will be dancing."

There were forty or fifty small round tables scattered around the perimeter of the room, each with a small shaded lamp in the center. Most of the tables were empty, but at a few of them people were sitting and eating. At one table a handsome young man had food in front of him, but he ignored it in favor of watching the dancers with his arms crossed. Others were browsing at a long buffet table. Almost everyone was in formal evening clothes.

"Who's that wrestling with Clair de Lune on the dance floor?" Polly asked Mr. Kepler.

"That's Bernard Cathcart."

"Is he somebody?"

"I believe he has money, Miss St. Jough."

"I suspect that everybody here tonight except us has more money than is good for them," True guessed. "Is this a charity function? Otto didn't say, but I wouldn't think Miss de Lune would need charity."

"Still, in a manner of speaking, that's what it is," Mr. Kepler said. "Mr. Windsor," he nodded at the unhappy young man sitting alone at one of the tiny tables, "and Miss de Lune are looking for people to invest in a new picture."

"I see. Well, let us at the buffet. We'd better eat before Otto remembers that I'm just a detective with limited resources."

Mr. Kepler laughed. "Have a nice dinner. Otto will speak to you soon."

True and Polly strolled across the room to the buffet table and began to put food on big plates. True accidentally bumped into a short chubby man with enormous features on a round deeply-lined face. "Excuse me," True said automatically, and then broke into a smile. "Freddy! Is that you? Look, Polly, Frederick Peregrine."

"I'm surprised you remember me. You haven't been down to the Fabulous Falcon Club in months."

"He's been busy detecting," Polly confided.

"Oh, yes," Peregrine said. "The two divas. I read all about it in the papers. That's no excuse."

"I suppose not," True said. "Interested in getting into pictures?"

Before Peregrine could answer, a woman wearing a dark blue business suit and practical shoes turned to them. "I am," she admitted in a good loud carrying voice. True, Polly, and Peregrine looked at her as if she were some new kind of animal.

"I'm Ruth Booth," the woman said, and waited as if she expected they would know her.

True did the honors from his side.

"Amos True, the detective!" Miss Booth exclaimed. "I've been reading about you in the papers. Very clever of you to figure out which diva was which."

"I feel sure I should know you, Miss Booth," Polly said, her forehead wrinkling with thought.

Miss Booth smiled. "I do my best to make it easy," she said. "I write books for children: The Get-Around

Family. It's a series."

"I don't have children myself," Polly admitted, "but I think I heard you being wise and witty on one of the late night shows."

"That's right."

"Shall we sit?" Mr. Peregrine suggested. "I think there will be enough room for all four of us if we push two of those tiny tables together."

"Very good," Miss Booth said. She took Mr. Peregrine's arm and steered him to an empty table. True and Polly followed. By the time they arrived, Miss Booth had pushed another table up to the first one. Even with two tables, the seating was intimate, and they had to be careful with their knees and elbows.

"Who is that man over there?" True asked. The man had very short hair, and his darkly tanned face was drawn, almost skeletal. He wore a sport coat, slacks, and a collared powder blue shirt without a tie. Before him was a plate of raw vegetables, which he picked up a piece at a time and nibbled on, rabbit-like.

"I don't know him," Mr. Peregrine said.

"I believe that's Art Field," Miss Booth said. "You know, of Field's Gyms?"

"You certainly are well-informed, Miss Booth," True said.

"I like to stay on top of things," she declared. "I live life."

"Certainly the best thing to live," Polly agreed.

"Yes," Miss Booth said as if she were unsure exactly what Polly meant by that.

"He doesn't look very happy to be here," True said as he nodded in the direction of Mr. Windsor.

"You can't please everybody," Miss Booth said.

CHAPTER THREE
TOO MANY FEELINGS

The music ended. Huffing and puffing, Mr. Cathcart escorted Clair de Lune back to the table where Mr. Windsor was sitting.

"Had enough, Clair?" Mr. Windsor asked.

"Oh, Brad," Miss de Lune said. "I think it was very kind of Mr. Cathcart to dance with me."

"Later," Mr. Windsor said, "I'll check you for finger-prints."

"What do you mean by that?" Mr. Cathcart retorted angrily.

"What do you think I mean?" Mr. Windsor replied. He stood up, apparently ready to do battle.

"How would you like a swift punch in the nose?" Mr. Cathcart asked.

True was about to go break up the rumpus, but it turned out not to be necessary.

Miss de Lune acted as peacemaker. "Sit down, both of you," she said as she waved at the waiters. "More drinks all around," she called out to them.

Both Mr. Cathcart and Mr. Windsor settled into their chairs, but they continued to glare at each other. The

tallest of the three waiters slouched across the dance floor—now empty—and took their orders. He was nearly bald, but had a gigantic mustache which twisted up at the ends.

"Let's dance," Mr. Windsor demanded. Miss de Lune seemed astonished as he pulled her out onto the floor. The band began to play, and Mr. Windsor guided her around to "All of Me." He was actually quite a good dancer. Miss de Lune whispered into his ear, and from the expression on Mr. Windsor's face, she wasn't whispering endearments.

They were still dancing when the tall mustachioed waiter returned with the drinks. He set down two gin and tonics, picked up the dirty glasses, and then managed to spill most of Mr. Cathcart's bourbon and soda into his lap. "You fool!" Mr. Cathcart shouted as he sprang to his feet, ineffectually brushing at himself with a napkin.

"Sorry, sir," the waiter said as if he were anything but. He hovered, but made no move to help.

Miss Núñez hurried in, led by one of the other waiters. She went directly to Mr. Cathcart and tried to calm him. She was good at it—promising to pay the cleaning bill, and to get him a new drink, and so on—and though he remained unhappy, she did manage to get a brave smile out of him.

"She's good," True remarked.

"It's a talent some of us have," Polly said.

The song ended, and Mr. Windsor and Miss de Lune returned to the table. Mr. Windsor smiled at Mr.

Cathcart. "Sorry about the drink, old boy," he said.

Mr. Cathcart only "harrumphed" at him, excused himself, and went to his stateroom to change.

Miss Núñez took the waiter, who she called Walter, into a corner and had a serious discussion with him. Walter did his best to look repentant. He said little but nodded a lot.

"Are you writing anything at the moment?" Mr. Peregrine asked Miss Booth.

"I'm in the midst of a new installment of The Get-Around Family," Miss Booth said. "Oh yes, in the midst. The working title is *The Dog Ate My Homework*." She shook her finger at True. "Maybe next time I'll write about a detective," she warned gaily.

"I'm sure Amos would be pleased to act as technical adviser," Polly said. "Isn't that right, Amos?"

"I'm not really very technical," True said. "Besides, I think running a night spot like the Fabulous Falcon Club would be a much more interesting subject."

"Would that be appropriate for a children's book?" Mr. Peregrine asked.

Miss Booth was about to answer, but she was distracted when a padded door at one side of the room opened allowing a man to emerge from whatever was beyond.

"Oh, Zoltan!" Miss Booth cried. "Over here."

Zoltan ambled to where the four of them were sitting. Miss Booth introduced him, and he made a stiff bow.

Polly gave him her brightest social smile.

"Good to see you again," True said.

Zoltan agreed that it was also good to see True and Polly.

Miss Booth tried to reorganize the party so there would be room for him to sit down, but he refused her kind offer. "I have just come from a dinner meeting with Mr. Laird," he explained. "And now I must arrange things for this evening's séance. I invite all of you, and the others too," he waved a dramatic hand at the guests at the other tables, "to join me at ten o'clock in the ship's museum."

"Zoltan is going to contact Captain Henry Robbins," Miss Booth confided.

"One can but try," Zoltan said. "Now, if you will excuse me…." He walked quickly from the room.

"Who is Captain Henry Robbins?" Mr. Peregrine asked.

"He commanded this ship before Mr. Laird bought it," Miss Booth explained. "I understand Captain Robbins was something of a pirate, and that lately he's been haunting the place."

Mr. Peregrine glanced around the big room anxiously. "You can't be serious."

"Mr. Laird was serious enough to hire Zoltan," True suggested.

"I wonder what he means by 'arrange things,'" Polly asked no one in particular.

"I'm sure he's just setting up chairs and so on," Miss Booth remarked.

"It's the 'and so on,' part that I am curious about," True said.

"Surely, you don't believe he's a fake," Mr. Peregrine asked hopefully.

"Surely, I don't know," True said. "But it is fun trying to guess."

Miss Booth and Mr. Peregrine considered True's comment. Then Miss Booth shook herself as if awakening from a dream. "A children's book about a nightclub?" she asked herself. She seemed to seriously consider the idea. "I don't know. I could make the place a malt shop, I suppose," she suggested.

"You think so?" Mr. Peregrine ask, relieved that the conversation had returned to a more comfortable topic.

"Come on, Polly," True said. "While they discuss literature, let's look around."

"I think you'd be good at writing children's books," Polly said as they walked out of Neptune's Hideaway.

"You're only saying that because you know I have the mind of a child," True replied.

They strolled arm in arm along the wide hallway in no particular hurry. Somewhere below engines thrummed. Since the ship wasn't going anywhere, they had to be generating the ship's electricity.

True paused at a door marked CREW ONLY, and Polly had to drag him away. Farther along they found a hole-in-the-wall bar where a man in a red coat was reading a magazine. When the bartender saw True and Polly, he quickly closed the magazine and slapped both hands on the bar—ready for business. "What'll you have?" he asked.

"Two gin and tonic," True told him. He and Polly

settled on stools.

"Private party," True said.

"Yes, sir," the man said.

"Lovely, place."

"Yes, sir."

"You like it here?"

"Oh yes, sir." He thought for a moment. "Except.…"

"Except what?" Polly asked.

The man dealt paper coasters with a drawing of a duck on each—certainly a lucky duck—and then served the drinks.

"Nothing," the man said.

"Nothing at all?" Polly asked.

"Well, nothing, except sometimes I hear things."

"I hear things, sometimes," Polly said. "For instance, right now I'm hearing you."

"Yes, ma'am," the bartender said.

They sipped their drinks while making further small talk with the bartender. When they got up to leave, True offered him money.

"No, sir," the bartender said. "It's all taken care of."

"You've been very pleasant," True said and left two dollars on the bar.

The bills went away and the bartender wished them luck.

"We don't gamble much," True told him.

"Everybody needs luck," the bartender said, and began to swab the bar with a rag.

"Nice man," Polly said as she and True continued their stroll. "Except he hears things."

"I was wondering about that."

"Why? What sorts of thing do you think he heard?"

True shrugged. "Whatever it was, he didn't want to talk about it. Maybe Otto can clear up the mystery."

"You think there's a connection between Otto's ghost and whatever that man has been hearing?"

"I don't think anything yet. I just have a feeling."

"That's why you never have a vacation," Polly said. "Too many feelings."

"Later on I'll lie down. Maybe the feeling will go away."

They passed the main casino, a long room paneled in dark wood, and furnished with craps tables, blackjack tables, a couple of roulette wheels, and a few rows of slot machines. A dealer stood behind each table, ready for customers. About halfway down the room a bartender waited behind a small bar with a padded edge. A hallway crossed beyond the far end.

The only dealer working at the moment was dealing blackjack to the only customer, a bored-looking older woman with a fox fur around her neck and too many bracelets. The bracelets clinked against each other when she moved. The dealer slapped down a card. The woman sighed and pushed across a small stack of chips. Despite the sigh, the loss didn't seem to upset her much.

"Do you know her?" Polly asked.

"Not yet," True said, and escorted Polly into the big quiet room. The dealers stood a little straighter. They watched True and Polly walk to where the woman was

sitting.

The woman looked up at them and tried an unsuccessful smile that somehow only made her look older. She smelled like dusty violets. True introduced himself and Polly.

"How do you do?" the woman said. "I'm Mrs. Cathcart."

"Oh yes," Polly said. "We met your husband at dinner."

"Good old Bernard," Mrs. Cathcart said. "Did he succeed in offending you? He's good at that."

"Not yet," True said. "He was busy."

"How are the cards running for you tonight?" Polly asked, deftly changing the subject.

"About usual for me," Mrs. Cathcart said.

Mr. Kepler joined them. "How are you tonight, Mrs. Cathcart?" he asked. He rested a hand on her shoulder, as if she were more than just another guest of the ship.

"Losing."

"Your luck is bound to change. Do you mind if I drag Mr. True and Miss St. Jough away?"

"Of course not. Bernard and the others will be along soon enough. I must enjoy my solitude while I can."

"Of course." Mr. Kepler nodded at Mrs. Cathcart and led True and Polly out of the room.

"She seems like a very unhappy woman," Polly said as they walked slowly down the hallway.

"She couldn't be anything else," Mr. Kepler said, "married to Bernard Cathcart." He said this with some venom.

"You know the Cathcarts well?" Polly asked.

"Well enough to dislike the husband," Mr. Kepler said. "He's here only because Miss de Lune and Mr. Windsor think he might be convinced to invest in their project."

"I've been meaning to ask somebody about that," True said. "Clair de Lune is a popular actress—the next big thing as they say. Why does she and her director need to collect donations to make a picture?"

Mr. Kepler smiled and shook his head. "It's like this, you see: The studio wants her to continue making silly romantic comedies, mostly because they bring in a lot of money. But Miss de Lune thinks of herself as a serious artist—and maybe she is. I wouldn't know. Anyway, she and Mr. Windsor want to make a picture with more substance. That's what the money is for."

"They're going to produce their own picture?" Polly asked. "How exciting."

"That's it," Mr. Kepler said. "Hooray for Hollywood, eh?"

"I hope the other guests have more money than I have," True said.

"They do," Mr. Kepler said. "Come on. I'll show you around."

"Very kind of you," True said.

"Not at all." Mr. Kepler winked at them. "Orders from Mr. Laird."

He took them out on deck, where fog had gathered around the ship like a heavy coat. Somewhere off to the right the bell of a buoy rang casually as it rocked

in the calm water. Even farther off a foghorn called mournfully.

"What happened to Santa Monica?" Polly asked as she peered into the fog.

"Right where we left it, I hope," True replied.

They watched the fog swirl for a moment or two, then Polly shivered and crossed her arms.

"Would you like to see the bridge?" Mr. Kepler asked.

"Is it inside?" Polly asked.

"Of course."

"Then yes, please," Polly said.

Mr. Kepler chuckled as he took them back inside, then up a companionway to a wide promenade lined with shops, all closed and dark at the moment. From there they caught an elevator. Mr. Kepler inserted a key and turned it. "Officially, the bridge is off limits to guests," he announced like a conspirator. The elevator shot them to the top, and the doors opened into a glassed-in hallway that curved around a large room containing a ship's wheel, several freestanding controls and instruments, and a pair of large tables on which charts could be unrolled. The room was lit by a single blue emergency light in the ceiling.

"The place could use a dusting," Polly remarked.

"Well," Kepler explained, "it doesn't get much use with the ship sitting in one place all the time."

They followed the hallway around the bridge. The outer windows gave them a good view of the fog, but not much else. "I'll take you up here during the day

sometime," Mr. Kepler promised. "When it's clear the view can be quite spectacular. If you've seen enough for the moment, I can take you back to the casino."

"I'd rather you took us to see Otto," True said.

"So would I," Mr. Kepler said. "But I have my orders."

"Come on," Polly said, and took True's arm. "I want to see if I can't get the best of one of those one-armed bandits."

CHAPTER FOUR
DANCING WITH THE CAPTAIN

Mr. Field sat at one of the blackjack tables, not playing, but observing with disapproval everything he saw. Walter, the bald waiter with the big mustache, stood next to the padded bar staring at Mr. Cathcart. Mr. Cathcart glanced over his shoulder at Walter a few times, but most of his attention remained on Miss de Lune. The two of them were playing blackjack, but not at the table where Mrs. Cathcart was sitting. Mrs. Cathcart sat with her back to them, but she certainly could not avoid hearing their laughter and their discussion of the game. "Oh, Mr. Cathcart," Miss de Lune remarked again and again.

Polly played a nickel slot while True played roulette. She broke about even, but True quickly lost twenty bucks playing a system he made up on the spot. "That'll teach you," Polly said. "How are you doing, Mr. Peregrine?"

Peregrine was standing across the table from True, and he had a large pile of chips in front of him. "Oh, all right, I guess," he said.

"You seem to be winning, anyway."

"One can't do better than that," True said.

Mr. Peregrine fixed Polly with a solemn eye. "Nobody wins all the time," he told her. "Places like this stay in business because people lose more than they win. I know. I used to run a joint like this."

"He must be talking about you, Amos," Polly said. "Maybe you should have played Mr. Peregrine's system instead of your own."

Before True had a chance to answer, they heard a whoop from the other side of the room. It was Ruth Booth. She was playing craps, and she seemed to be winning.

"How are you doing, Miss Booth?" Polly called over to her.

"Fine," she called back enthusiastically. "But win or lose, I'm enthralled."

Clair de Lune strolled over to Miss Booth, with Mr. Cathcart skulking close behind. "If you win enough," she said, "you can invest in my picture. Mr. Windsor and I want to make one of George Eliot's novels, *The Mill on the Floss*. I'm going to play Maggie Tulliver."

"It's really a wonderful romantic story," Mr. Cathcart assured Miss Booth. "I'm going to invest, myself."

"I'm sure it is, Mr. Cathcart." Miss Booth frowned. "I think I was forced to read it in college. Have you spoken to Mr. True about your project, Miss de Lune? Famous detectives are made of money, you know."

Warily, True watched Miss de Lune approach. By the time she stood before him, Brad Windsor had wandered over to the roulette table and was trying

to remain inconspicuous. Mr. Cathcart hovered at the edge of the crowd, waiting for another chance to astound Miss de Lune.

"Miss Booth tells me that you're a private detective," Miss de Lune said.

"She also tells you that I'm made of money. She's wrong about that."

"He's too honest to be rich," Polly explained.

Both Mr. Windsor and Mr. Cathcart made noises of disbelief.

"Well, I'm fascinated anyway," Miss de Lune said. "Even if you can't invest."

"I'm not sure I would invest in your movie even if I had the money," True admitted.

"Why not, Mr. True?" Miss de Lune seemed genuinely mystified.

"Like Miss Booth I did my time reading *The Mill on the Floss*. I don't believe a modern audience is ready for all the excitement. Of course, that's just my opinion."

"I can't always tell when you're serious," Miss de Lune said.

"You're not alone," Polly said. She introduced herself to Miss de Lune and shook her hand. "I can tell you the truth about him. He's too honest to be rich, but not too honest to inflate his experiences a little when he talks about them."

"Why, Polly," True said, sounding a little insulted.

Polly and Miss de Lune strolled off with their heads together.

"Well, can you beat that?" Mr. Cathcart said.

"Women," Mr. Windsor remarked crossly.

Mr. Cathcart and Mr. Windsor looked at each other suspiciously and walked off in opposite directions, leaving True and Mr. Peregrine alone at the roulette table. Across the way Miss Booth shrieked happily again.

"Are you going to put any money into their picture?" True asked Mr. Peregrine.

"I may. But first I'd have to hear a lot more details. For one thing, I'd have to know who was writing the screenplay."

"Not George Eliot," True told him. "She's dead."

"She may be the lucky one," Mr. Peregrine replied.

True could only agree.

Miss Núñez marched into the casino and made an announcement. "Ladies and gentlemen, in ten minutes, Zoltan will attempt to contact the ghost of Captain Henry Robbins in the ship's museum on B Deck. You are all invited to participate."

"Participate?" Mr. Peregrine asked fearfully.

Miss Núñez smiled at him. "Or merely observe," she assured him.

"Come on, Miss Booth," True said, "we wouldn't want to miss the first apparition." Miss Booth began a rambling story about the supernatural experiences she'd had. The others straggled after. Mr. Cathcart and Mr. Windsor each did his best to escort Miss de Lune while ignoring the other gentleman. Mr. Peregrine graciously took Mrs. Cathcart's arm.

Polly caught up with True and Miss Booth. They and

the others followed Miss Núñez up to B Deck, along a corridor, and into a large space that may once have been four or five staterooms. In the center of the room was an enormous round table—big enough for King Arthur and his knights—with sufficient chairs for all the invited guests, plus an extra one for Zoltan himself. Zoltan was already seated. With his eyes closed and his hands flat on the table top he took no notice of the entering crowd.

On the walls were posters advertising world cruises, and cases full of souvenirs of the various people who'd owned the *Lucky Duck* before Otto Laird: dinnerware, uniforms, lengths of chain and line. In one corner stood an enormous anchor with decorative clumps of barnacles all over it. Hanging on the wall over the anchor was a painting of a rather piratical-looking gentleman with long hair, chin whiskers, and mismatched uniform hat, coat, and pants.

Polly studied the painting. "Could this be our guest of honor?" she asked.

"Yes, indeed," Miss Núñez said. "That is Captain Henry Robbins. He owned the *Lucky Duck* just before Mr. Laird. In Captain Robbins' day the ship was called the *Hippocampus*. They say he was something of a smuggler."

"He certainly looks the part," Miss de Lune said.

Miss Núñez agreed.

Mr. Kepler joined the group that had gathered around the portrait. "Mr. True," he said, "here is a display that might be of interest to someone in your business."

He led True to a case hung from the wall. The others tagged along. Inside the case were flintlock rifles and one shot cap-and-ball pistols right alongside revolvers and modern automatics. Among them was a selection of useful-looking knives. Mr. Kepler used a key to turn off an alarm—"It's a terrible noise," he assured them. "You wouldn't want to hear it."—and opened the case. He handed one of the pistols to True, who stuck it into his belt and struck a piratical pose. Everyone but Mr. Field and Mrs. Cathcart laughed appreciatively.

"You ought to get one of those," Polly advised. "It will impress the clients."

"Impressing you is all that concerns me, my dear." True gave the weapon back to Mr. Kepler. "Some of these weapons look to be very old, maybe seventeenth century," True said. "The *Lucky Duck* isn't more than fifty years old at most."

"Correct," Mr. Kepler said. "I understand the captain was something of a history buff. He fancied himself a pirate of the old school and used the old weapons and equipment whenever he could."

"A stickler for authenticity, eh?" Miss Booth suggested.

"That's our boy, the captain," Mr. Kepler agreed.

"If you will all be seated," Miss Núñez called. She was standing to the right and a little behind Zoltan.

Everyone but Mr. Peregrine found a seat at the big round table.

"Won't you join us?" Miss Núñez asked.

Everybody was looking at Mr. Peregrine. He was

sweating, and he glanced around the room as if he thought the captain might burst out from behind one of the exhibits. At last he gave a jerky nod and took an empty chair next to Miss Booth. She patted his hand and smiled at him reassuringly.

Zoltan's eyes popped open and he stared straight ahead. "Good evening," he said. "Please join hands with the person on either side of you."

They did so.

"Now, I must tell you that this experiment in communication requires that all of you clear your minds of antagonistic thoughts. It would be best if you did not have any thoughts of your own at all. Allow the infinite to guide you entirely."

"That should be easy enough for some of us," Mr. Windsor said.

"Brad," Miss de Lune warned.

"Please restrain your attempts at levity," Zoltan said.

"Would you like me to turn the lights down?" Miss Núñez asked. She was standing by the control at the door.

"That will not be necessary," Zoltan said. "But do close the door. We do not wish to be disturbed at this delicate juncture. Now, everyone: please clear your minds." While he waited for their minds to clear, True winked at Polly and she winked back. Soon Zoltan continued: "We come to you as suppliants seeking knowledge. If there are any here who would speak to us, give us a sign."

A long time seemed to pass. There was a sudden

knocking that seemed to come from all around them, and everyone but Zoltan jumped as if touched with a live electric wire.

On True's left, Polly was squeezing his hand hard. Mr. Peregrine was doing the same on his right. Polly's hand was dry. Mr. Peregrine's was slick with sweat.

Zoltan rocked in his chair when suddenly a long-suffering moan came out of nowhere and echoed as it filled the room. At first True thought that somehow the foghorn had drifted alongside the *Lucky Duck*, though that did not seem possible. When the moan came again, it sounded more as if someone were dying in the ventilation system.

Polly squeezed tighter. Mr. Peregrine was not the only person at the table who was terrified.

"If you are Captain Robbins, moan again," Zoltan said.

On the wall a few yards behind Zoltan was a heavy wall-hanging of the *Lucky Duck* in heavy seas—or the *Hippocampus*, as it was called when Henry Robbins was captain. Someone was standing in front of it, fists on hips, legs spread—Captain Henry Robbins.

Nobody moved.

The captain moaned again and pulled his saber.

Mrs. Cathcart, began to scream hysterically and went on as if she would never stop. Polly pulled away from True, hurried over to Mrs. Cathcart, and tried to calm her. Mrs. Cathcart continued screaming, and then broke down in heavy sobbing tears. Keeping a careful eye on the captain, Miss Booth got a glass of water

from an array on a side table and hurriedly brought it to them, but Mrs. Cathcart was too upset to drink it. Polly took a few sips.

Captain Robbins laughed unpleasantly, like water gurgling down a drain, and ducked behind the wall hanging. True was after him immediately. As he'd expected, behind the wall-hanging True found a door that opened onto a corridor.

He paused in the corridor for only a second, long enough to get his bearings, and saw the captain running toward Neptune's Hideaway. True followed like a shot. The captain was in sight till he rounded a corner.

True was no more than three or four seconds behind him, but when he arrived at the corner the corridor was empty. True hurried along looking for a place where the captain might be hiding. He passed a door marked CREW ONLY, found that it was unlocked, and stepped over the combing to find himself at the top of a metal stairway that lead down into a dim stairwell lit only occasionally by emergency lights. Quick heavy footsteps ran below him. True started down and the stairway rang as he leaped two or three steps at a time.

When True reached the bottom of the stairwell at last, he found a large, badly lit industrial space—certainly the ship's hold. The few emergency lights served only to make the gloom seem more creepy. The place had the combined smell of old standing water, ancient machine oil, and a suggestion of every cargo it had ever carried. The thrumming of the engines made the whole hold vibrate. It was easy to believe the place

was haunted. True shivered, only partly from the cold.

He pulled a pen flashlight from his coat pocket and shone it around. In the spotlight he found a rat drinking from a shallow puddle; it looked up at him, chittered angrily, and scampered off.

The captain had run through the puddle, and True was able to follow his footsteps a few feet into the big dark space. Crates and bales were stacked all around. Some of the containers might hold booze or canned hash or virgin decks of cards for the customers upstairs. Some could have been left behind by previous tenants, maybe by the captain himself. When the wet footsteps faded out, True stopped and listened. On top of the base note of the engine thrum was the movement of tiny creatures. Paper crinkled.

Quietly, carefully, True moved toward the paper noise, but in the enormous room it was difficult to tell from which direction it came. True walked until he struck the side of the hold, and followed it past a white rectangular box the size of a small room, with a badge on it that indicated it was a refrigerator.

Farther on walls divided the deck, and True stopped to listen. A few seconds later the paper rattle came again, and True followed it down a narrow corridor. There were doors on either side. He tried one of them and it was locked. A few yards down a door was open and from inside bright light poured out into the corridor. True looked around the edge of the doorway and saw a man in dungarees and a t-shirt sitting on an ancient cane-back chair reading a newspaper through

half-glasses.

True backed away into the darkness, and sneaked off to where another corridor crossed the one he was in. He stopped to listen and heard a noise that might have been shuffling feet or might have just been a particularly large rat trying to get comfortable.

Moving as silently as he could, True hurried along the dark corridor following the round patch of light from his pen flash. He stopped more than once to listen, to find out if anything had changed. The shuffling kept moving. It was now well over to one side. The captain was dancing with him. True had to make sure the captain didn't get behind him with that saber, or maybe with one of those pistols he favored. True walked to where two corridors intersected and waited, his back against the corridor wall, for the captain to come to him.

He waited for what seemed like a long time for the shuffling to get closer. The captain seemed to be just wandering around. This gave True time to wrap his coat around his arm so he could use it to block the saber, should that be necessary. At last True heard the shuffling come very close and stop. He was sure the captain was just around the corner. True wished he had a gun, but it hadn't seemed that visiting the *Lucky Duck* required one. All he could do was surprise the captain and hope for the best. True leaped around the corner and grabbed the captain.

A woman shrieked in a voice that was somehow familiar.

True jumped back and shined the light of his pen flash on his victim. "Miss Booth," True exclaimed.

She was leaning against a wall and breathing hard, her hand to her throat. "My, that was exciting," she said between gasps.

"Are you all right?" True asked. "What are you doing down here?"

"I'll be fine in a moment," Miss Booth said.

True waited for an explanation.

"When you chased Captain Robbins, I chased you. I can't sit in my room typing all the time. I need to live life! I must have experiences!"

"You and Hemingway," True suggested.

"Er, yes. Mostly, I wanted to watch a real detective in action. I thought I might be able to help. Before I started writing children's books, I wrote scenarios for the pictures: the Walt Woo mystery series."

"I always loved the Woos. Though I found most of the plots pretty unlikely."

"Realism was never my strength." She laughed. "Which I suppose was one of the reasons they hired me."

The man who'd been reading the paper stood in the middle of the corridor, clutching his reading material in one fist. "No guests allowed down here," he informed them grumpily.

"We were just leaving," True said. He took Miss Booth's arm and firmly steered her back to the metal stairway.

"But we haven't found the captain," Miss Booth

said, moving under protest.

"And we're not likely to after all the noise we've been making."

"Oh. You're right, of course. That obviously wasn't a real ghost."

"Obviously."

"The question is, was it really Captain Robbins?"

"I doubt it," True said.

"Then who—?"

"I don't know," True said. "But when I see Mr. Laird at last, that is one of the first questions I'll ask him."

When True and Miss Booth returned to the museum, they found the place empty except for Polly, Clair de Lune, and Brad Windsor sitting at the big round table. Everybody else, including Zoltan and Miss Núñez, was gone.

Polly stared at the cards she held fanned in her hands. "Do you have any fives?" she asked Miss de Lune.

"Go fish," Miss de Lune said.

Polly took the deck's top card and stared at it without joy.

Mr. Windsor put down his cards and looked expectantly at True.

"Do you think that moaning is what the bartender heard?" Polly asked.

"Probably," True said. "If so, he'll be glad to learn that he wasn't imagining things. Where is everybody?"

"You missed the mass exodus," Polly said. "As soon as you were gone, everybody—well almost everybody—decided they had better things to do than attend

a party on a haunted ship. They've all gone to pack."

"Didn't they know about the ghost before they came?" True asked. "Why did they think Zoltan was here?"

"Seeing is believing," Brad Windsor said.

"They thought Captain Robbins was very convincing," Miss de Lune told True. She shook her head. "I don't think any of them will invest in our movie now," she went on sadly.

"Amazing how effective a little moaning and a fright wig can be," True said. He studied the pitcher of water on the side table, and frowned.

"Did you find him?" Mr. Windsor asked. "The captain or whoever it was."

"Well, no," True admitted. "But I had help." He glanced at Miss Booth meaningfully. She got busy squaring up a deck of cards. "Just for the record," True went on, "I also do not believe for a moment that Captain Robbins is a ghost. But I think I need to discuss what happened this evening with Zoltan."

CHAPTER FIVE
ZOLTAN EXPLAINS

Polly followed True out of the room, and they marched down the hallway together. "You just can't ignore a mystery, can you?" she accused.

"I've tried and tried," he said despairingly.

"That's why I love you," Polly said. "You keep trying."

Mr. Kepler emerged from the rabbit warren where the executives had their offices and approached them eagerly. "I heard about what happened at the séance," he said. "What do you think?"

"I think," said True, "Zoltan and I have a lot to talk about."

"May I tag along?" Mr. Kepler asked.

"Of course," True said.

They visited Neptune's Hideaway and the main casino, but both were empty. "He must be in his stateroom," Mr. Kepler said.

True nodded. On a ship that size the possibility that Zoltan was in his stateroom seemed likely but far from certain.

Mr. Kepler led them along corridors for what seemed

to be a few city blocks, and at last came to Zoltan's door. Kepler bowed to True, indicating that he should do the honors. True knocked briskly.

"Who is it?" Zoltan asked through the door. He did not sound as if he really wanted to know.

"Amos True and friends," True announced. "Mr. Laird introduced us at lunch."

Zoltan opened the door and looked out at them. He had loosened his tie, and though he looked like his usual chipper self at the museum séance an hour or so before, he now looked haggard—as if he hadn't slept in weeks. Listlessly he invited them in.

"I suppose you want to talk about the séance," he said as he settled into a chair at a small desk. On the desk was a bottle and a glass with a splash of brown liquid in it.

"You *are* psychic, aren't you?" True said, and Polly slapped him on the arm. They were sitting on the end of Zoltan's bed.

"I assume you know that what we saw was a person in a costume, not a ghost," Zoltan said. "What else do you wish to know?" He sounded very tired.

"You may consider it impolite to ask," True said, "but I want to make sure that the captain's appearance was not something you two had cooked up between you beforehand."

"It *is* impolite," Zoltan said. "But I am accustomed to such questions. The answer is 'no.' I was as surprised as any of you when the captain arrived. And I did not prepare the room in any way except for requesting the

round table and the chairs. As you may recall, when Miss Núñez asked if she should turn down the lights, I asked that she not do so."

True nodded, but it was a slow thoughtful nod.

"Now I have a question for *you*, Mr. True."

"I'll answer it if I can," True said.

"I understand that you chased after the captain when he hurriedly left the room. Did you learn anything more useful than the fact that I might be a charlatan?"

"The captain headed for the hold of the ship, but I did not find him down there. Of course, there are plenty of places to hide, and there are probably exits I know nothing about. He could be anywhere by now."

"And have you any guesses why this person is masquerading as Captain Robbins?"

"None whatsoever," True said.

"Neither do I," Zoltan said, and drank the last of the brown liquid in his glass.

"There you are, Amos," Polly said. "The final word from Zoltan."

True looked at her with surprise and almost smiled.

Mr. Kepler made a short explosive laugh. He was leaning against the door with his arms crossed. "I have one question, if I may," he said.

"Certainly," True said. "If it is all right with Zoltan."

Zoltan shrugged.

"Do you really believe," Mr. Kepler said, "that you could have summoned up the captain if the intruder hadn't beaten you to it?"

"I have faith in my talent," Zoltan said. "But a

successful summoning of a presence from the Other Side requires great concentration and a little luck. Not all spirits hover near at all times. Under this evening's unusual circumstances, I don't think anyone could have contacted Captain Robbins or any other spirit."

They were all still considering Zoltan's explanation when a scream that was full of fear came from somewhere down the hall and they all jumped. Mr. Kepler leaped out of the way as True and Miss St. Jough ran for the doorway.

CHAPTER SIX
TRUE TAKES CHARGE

The scream came again. True and Polly followed the fading sound along the hallway to one of the staterooms. Mr. Kepler followed a few steps behind. Walter, the bald waiter with the big mustache, stood just inside the open door. One of the maids stood near him, eyes wide with fear, her hands to her face. Beyond her, in a puddle of blood, a man lay on the floor with a knife in his chest.

Polly, Miss Booth, Miss de Lune, Mr. Windsor, and Mr. Kepler bunched up behind True. "What is it?" Miss Booth asked enthusiastically. When she saw the body, she said, "Oh," and her expression sagged.

Otto Laird, now wearing a tuxedo, hurried up. "Is there a problem?" he asked.

"Hello, Otto," True said. "Glad you could make it."

"Good to see you too, True," Mr. Laird said. "Sorry I've been so busy. You'd be surprised the amount of paperwork it takes to keep this place running."

"You will have more paperwork after this," True said. "Among your exhibits and attractions you now can claim a genuine murder victim."

Mr. Laird nodded to Polly, then did a double-take. "Murder?" he asked, surprised. When he saw for himself the tableau in the stateroom his eyes narrowed. "I'm glad you're here, True."

"One might almost suspect you'd planned this for my entertainment," True said.

"What? Why, I assure you—"

"You can stop sputtering, Otto," True said, interrupting him. "It was a bad joke." He turned to Polly and suggested she take the maid away. "See if she knows anything useful," he whispered to her.

Polly nodded and gently helped the maid out of the stateroom.

True turned to the waiter with the bald head and the big mustache. "What about you?" he asked.

"What *about* me?" the waiter said.

"I hear your name is Walter."

"Yes, Walter Peevy. But that's no crime."

"I guess not," True agreed. "What were you doing here?"

"I was delivering food that Mr. Cathcart had ordered. If you don't believe me, you can ask about it in the kitchen."

"I believe you," True assured him. "Say, aren't you the fellow who spilled a drink on Mr. Cathcart in Neptune's Hideaway?"

"I am."

"Well, well," True commented.

"What does that mean?" Walter asked irritably.

"Nothing much. Just taking note. You can go. See

that you don't leave the ship."

Walter Peevy nodded and hurried away.

True went into the stateroom and the crowd surged forward. "Miss Booth, can you keep everyone out of here while I search for clues?"

"What about me?" Mr. Laird asked.

"Let Mr. Laird in if he promises not to touch anything."

Taking the job very seriously, Miss Booth blocked the door and folded her arms.

True knelt next to the body of Bernard Cathcart. The knife in his chest was really more of a fancy dagger decorated all over with trails of gold. It had a gently curved blade and was a little less a foot long.

"Otto, will you look in the bathroom to see if Mr. Cathcart used talcum powder? I doubt we'll find fingerprints on the murder weapon, but I think we should check."

Mr. Laird went into the bathroom for a moment and returned with a can of talc. True sprinkled a small mound into his hand and carefully blew it onto the handle of the dagger. Nothing stuck, and True made an impolite noise. Using a clean handkerchief, he pulled the knife from the body, wrapped the handkerchief around it, and put it into his inside coat pocket.

"Mr. Laird?"

True looked toward the door and saw Miss Núñez trying to get past Miss Booth. Mr. Laird went to the door. "What is it, Miss Núñez?"

"It's Mr. Fields and Mrs. Cathcart: they insist on

leaving. They're out on the landing stage waiting for a water taxi."

"Captain Robbins again?"

"I'm afraid so, sir. I knew you'd want to speak to them before they left, so I told the pilots to wait for a word from me before they transport anyone back to Santa Monica."

"I think it would be a good idea if nobody left the ship until we straighten this out," True said.

"Straighten what out?" Miss Núñez asked.

"We've had an unscheduled murder," True said, and moved so Miss Núñez could see the body.

Miss Núñez got pale, and her eyes opened wide. True heard a short intake of breath.

"Are we all suspects, then, Mr. True?" Miss de Lune asked.

"Suspects, persons of interest, witnesses, the whole happy round."

"I love it," Miss Booth said and chuckled to herself.

"I don't love it," Mr. Windsor said in his usual charming fashion. "I was in the museum with Miss de Lune and Miss St. Jough while the murder was being committed. None of us could have done it."

"No, not while you were in the museum," True agreed. "But Polly and Mr. Kepler and I were speaking to Zoltan for a few minutes after that. Any of you had plenty of time to come here from the museum and do the deed."

"That may be so," Mr. Windsor said accusingly. "But you're no policeman. You have no right to keep

us here."

"That's correct—I am not a policeman," True said. "But at the moment we are not in California—some authorities say that beyond the three-mile limit as we are, we're not even in the United States. The police have no more jurisdiction here than I do. Mr. Laird, an old buddy, has asked me to help out. I guess that makes me sort of semi-official. I'd take it as a personal favor if you stay around for questioning. You might know something you didn't know you knew."

"Something I didn't know I knew," Mr. Windsor said with disgust. "Come on, Clair," he continued as he turned away. "Let's go chain ourselves to the walls of our staterooms."

As she hurried to catch up with Mr. Windsor, Miss de Lune apologized for his attitude.

"Quite all right," True said.

"As you know, Mr. Windsor is not the only guest who feels that way," Miss Núñez assured him.

True shrugged. "I don't mean to be irritating, but sometimes I can't help myself," he said. "I'll go talk to Mr. Fields and Mrs. Cathcart. I'm already the bad guy."

"Of course, True. Anything you say." Mr. Laird glanced in the direction of the body. "What do we do with, er, him?"

"I believe you have a refrigerator down in the hold," True said. "Get somebody to put him in there until we can transport him back to the mainland for autopsy and burial—whatever the police and the family decide.

Meanwhile, lock this room. I may have missed a clue. Let's go, Miss Núñez."

Miss Núñez escorted True back out on deck, where Polly caught up with them. They passed the three water taxi pilots who were standing at the rail smoking and talking quietly. On a table nearby was a carafe of coffee, a plate of sandwiches, and three used cups.

"What news?" Moe asked. His name was squiggled in thread on his jacket.

"Yeah," Jack said, "we hear somebody was murdered." He pronounced it "moided."

"That's right," True said. "Know anything about it?"

"The ghost of Captain Robbins did it," Manny said. He and the other two pilots laughed.

"Don't you gentlemen believe in ghosts?" Polly asked.

"Not very much," Manny said. "Though I hear that the captain has a good reason for haunting the *Lucky Duck*."

"What is that?" True asked.

"The captain was a smuggler, you know," Manny began. "Yessiree, bob: Booze, fancy cheese, weapons, the occasional work of art—anything that he could acquire cheap and sell dear. For a few years, back when the *Lucky Duck* was called the *Hippocampus*, he roved up and down the coast between Canada and Mexico, the most famous pirate of his time—though he felt he had been born late: the golden age of piracy had been over for a while."

"Mr. Kepler showed us his weapons," Polly said.

"Yessiree, bob," Manny said. "He was quite a collector."

"The murder weapon looks as if it might have come from his collection," True said.

"Does it now?" Moe exclaimed, obviously impressed.

"That would fit right into the stories I've heard about him," Manny said. "After a while the crew came to believe that the captain was more interested in his collection than he was in piracy. So one night the first mate—a Mr. Gibbs, I believe—led a mutiny. The captain hid out in the secret rooms and passages he had designed to hide the booty or even himself if that became necessary. Well, it became necessary. He'd emerge now and then to knock off one of the crew, but he did it one time too many and eventually Gibbs and his men got him." Manny shook his head. "Yes, siree, bob," he went on, "I hear tell that he's haunting the ship because he's just not resting easy, you know? In his addled ghostly state he thinks that anybody aboard the ship is a friend of Gibbs—you know, a mutineer—and wants to do away with them."

"What happened to Gibbs and the others?" Polly asked.

"Some say they abandoned ship, joined the dry land criminal community. Others say that the ghost of the captain picked 'em off one by one."

"That all happened a long time ago," True noted. "Have you heard of any murders on board lately— before tonight?"

"I have not. These days he only scares people off.

But as I say, the captain is kind of addled. I guess he could start killing again at any time." Manny shrugged. "Personally, I've never seen anything like a secret passage, nor a ghost neither." He nodded at Mr. Field and Mrs. Cathcart waiting at the far edge of the landing stage. "Look at 'em out there freezing their tootsies off," he said. "It don't take much to scare some people."

"Yes, siree, bob," Polly agreed.

"Thanks for the history lesson," True said. "And by the way, you're not to take anyone back to Santa Monica until you get the okay from me."

"Just you?" Jack asked.

"Just me."

"We work for Mr. Laird," Jack pointed out.

"So do I," True said. "I'm running the investigation."

"All right," Manny said. "We get paid by the hour whether we're actually piloting a taxi or not."

"What do you think of Manny's story?" Miss Núñez asked as the three of them strolled along the deck to the gangplank.

"A little something for the tourists," Polly suggested.

"Yessiree, bob," True said, "Manny is quite a philosopher. How's the maid?" he asked, changing the subject as they descended the gangplank.

"Her name is Miss Ogden. I gave her a couple of aspirin, which I told her were sleeping pills, and she dropped right off."

"Naughty. Did she tell you anything interesting before you drugged her?"

"Not much. She is a strong believer in vengeful ghosts."

"I see. We should introduce her to Manny."

"But she did tell me that she saw Walter Peevy hanging around. Do you think that means anything?"

"Not according to him. But I like him, or most anybody else, for the guilty party more than I like Miss Ogden's theory that a ghost killed Mr. Cathcart."

They walked out onto the landing stage, where Mrs. Cathcart and Mr. Fields were standing among their luggage, kept warm by impatience. The water taxies were moored nearby, bobbing in the water.

"Good evening," Miss Núñez said. "I believe you know Mr. True and Miss St. Jough."

"What of it?" Mr. Field said, in no mood for polite conversation.

"There's been a murder," True said, "and until we find the culprit no one leaves the ship."

"Oh, is that so?" Mr. Field exclaimed and was about to release a torrent of angry words when he was interrupted by Mrs. Cathcart.

"Who is dead?" Mrs. Cathcart asked fearfully.

"I'm sorry to be the one to tell you," True said, "but it was your husband."

Mrs. Cathcart surprised them all by opening her mouth wide and letting loose a loud hysterical laugh, one that had been pent up and a long time coming. "This calls for a drink," she said at last.

"That's an unusual response," Polly said.

"I didn't like him very much," Mrs. Cathcart replied.

"But there is nothing unusual in that. A lot of people didn't like Bernard—most of the people who knew him, I suppose."

"I barely knew the man," Mr. Field said. "Certainly I didn't know him well enough to think about killing him. You have no right to keep me or anybody else here. You aren't the police."

"You are correct," True said. He went on to explain once again why he was standing in for the official constabulary. Field and Mrs. Cathcart gave him the usual arguments, but at last they agreed to return to the ship.

"I'll get someone to carry your bags to your staterooms," Miss Núñez said.

When everyone was once again safely aboard the *Lucky Duck*, True told Miss Núñez that it was past time he had a good sit down talk with Mr. Laird.

"He's probably hiding out in his office," Miss Núñez said. She smiled. "Well, you know what I mean. If you'll follow me?"

CHAPTER SEVEN
THE TURKISH DAGGER

True and Polly were surprised when Miss Núñez led them back to Neptune's Hideaway. The band was gone, and a bartender stood behind the bar polishing a glass that would never get any shinier while watching Mr. Field and Mrs. Cathcart, who were drinking at separate tables. Neither of them looked up when Miss Núñez led True and Polly across the floor to the padded door at the far side of the room through which Zoltan had emerged earlier that evening.

Miss Núñez opened the padded door, allowing True and Polly to enter a tiny room barely large enough for the three of them. At the other end was another padded door. "This little room insulates Mr. Laird's office from the noise in the nightclub—when there is noise." Her voice sounded flat and without emotion in the sound-proofed room. On the other side of the second padded door was a small waiting room paneled in dark wood. A rubber plant stood among the red leather chairs and magazines. Miss Núñez knocked on the door marked PRIVATE in gold letters.

"Come in," came Mr. Laird's voice.

The three of them went in and found Mr. Kepler standing before Mr. Laird's big paper-littered desk between two chairs that matched the chairs in the waiting room. Brass fixtures lit the big room, adding sheen to the wood-paneling. Other chairs and a couch were lined up along the walls. Paintings of magnificent ships under full sail hung here and there.

"I'm glad you've come," Mr. Laird said. "Mr. Kepler and I were just discussing the murder. Any theories yet?"

"Some people think it was the ghost of Captain Robbins," Polly said.

Mr. Kepler looked to True for confirmation.

"It's a theory," True said. "I don't have a better one right now."

"As you know we cannot involve the police in this," Mr. Laird said. "Therefore, Mr. True is acting on my behalf. He is in charge of the investigation. Cooperate with him any way you can."

"Yes, sir," Mr. Kepler said.

"Uh, sir," Miss Núñez said, "some of our guests are upset that they can't leave the ship."

"I can't do anything about that," Mr. Laird said. "Try to keep them happy. Jolly them along. Free drinks for all. You know what I mean. You're the expert."

"Yes, sir."

"Now, both of you get out of here. I need to talk to Mr. True and Miss St. Jough."

Miss Núñez turned to go, but Mr. Kepler just stared at him, surprised by the abrupt dismissal. "Was there

something, Mr. Kepler?" Mr. Laird asked.

"What about Zoltan?" Mr. Kepler asked.

"What about him?" Laird asked irritably. "He's a guest, and I suppose a suspect—like everybody else on board."

"Of course, sir." Mr. Kepler didn't look happy, but he followed Miss Núñez to the door and out of the room.

When Mr. Kepler and Miss Núñez were gone, Mr. Laird invited True and Polly to sit. He seemed to deflate as he collapsed back into his chair and sighed. True and Polly waited politely for him to begin, but he seemed to have forgotten they were there.

"Mr. Laird?" Polly said.

Mr. Laird sat up straighter, and shook his head. "I didn't know there was going to be a murder, and I didn't invite you and Miss St. Jough out here just to invest in Miss de Lune's moving picture." He gave them a sad smile. "Actually," he went on, "I called you because I was hoping you could figure out who or what was haunting the *Lucky Duck*."

"What about Zoltan? I thought that's why he was here," True said.

"Yes," Mr. Laird said, "But I was hoping that if both of you were here, one of you, each working in his own way, could solve the Captain Robbins mystery. But apparently it is not to be."

"Well, it's early yet," Polly said.

"Your wish may be granted," True said. "It is possible that the murder and the haunting are connected."

"You can't mean you believe that Captain Robbins

killed Bernard Cathcart."

"That's right. I can't. Manny, one of your water taxi pilots, filled us in on the captain's background. Nothing he said explains why the captain might have a special dislike for Bernard Cathcart."

"Yes, I've heard Manny's story," Mr. Laird said. "It might even be factual. Some of it. A little of it."

"You don't really believe the captain killed Mr. Cathcart," Polly said.

"I don't know what to believe. At first I thought the ghost was just a person dressed up as Captain Robbins. But the captain comes and goes and leaves nothing behind—just as if he were a real ghost."

"Manny spoke of secret passages," True said.

"'Yessiree, bob,' as Manny would say. I've heard about the passages too. They would explain how the ghost comes and goes so easily. But I've been all over the ship, and I've never found a secret passage."

"Quite a conundrum," True remarked. "The only other possibility is that some live person on this ship is a murderer."

"Who do you suspect?" Mr. Laird asked.

"No one in particular just yet. Mr. Cathcart was not very popular."

"You just watch," Polly said confidently. "Amos will figure it all out eventually."

"Sooner than that, I hope," True said. "I need to start interviewing suspects and witnesses—though telling one from the other may be a problem. Otto, would you have Mr. Kepler meet us in Neptune's Hideaway? I'd

like to start by asking him a few questions."

"Of course," Mr. Laird said. He was picking up his telephone receiver as True and Polly strolled from his office.

"I don't mind helping Otto," True said when they briefly stopped in the airlock between the two padded doors, "but I don't want to make solving his problems my life's work. I don't want to remain on this barge any longer than the other guests do."

Polly shook her head. "We shouldn't have left those dirty dishes in the sink," she said.

When they entered Neptune's Hideaway, Walter Peevy was looming over Mrs. Cathcart. They were deep in conversation. When Mrs. Cathcart saw True and Polly, she spoke up loudly. "Yes," she said, "a gin and tonic will be fine. Thank you for the suggestion." Walter bowed himself away from the table and went to the bar to fill Mrs. Cathcart's drink order.

Clair de Lune and Brad Windsor were sitting at a table with Ruth Booth and Mr. Peregrine. Miss Booth called out to True. He and Polly pulled up a couple of chairs and sat down with the group.

"Have you solved the crime yet?" Mr. Peregrine asked earnestly.

"I'm afraid I am still in the clue collecting phase of the operation," True said. "Perhaps one of you has a theory."

"My theory is good riddance," Brad Windsor said.

Miss de Lune slapped him on the arm. "Stop that, Brad. Mr. True will think you killed him."

"It's no secret that I didn't like him," Mr. Windsor said. "And it's also no secret that I wasn't alone in my feelings."

"I'm still rooting for the ghost," Miss Booth said.

"You believe in ghosts?" Polly asked.

"Not as ghosts *qua* ghosts. But I do believe that a live person will masquerade as a ghost if there's something in it for him."

"For instance?" Polly prompted.

"For instance, if Mr. Laird hired somebody to act like a ghost—for the entertainment value, you know."

"I'm afraid you have the wrong end of that stick, Miss Booth," True said. "Ever since the ghost appeared Mr. Laird has been losing business."

"Well then," said Miss Booth, a little flustered, "a competitor of Mr. Laird could have done the hiring."

"It's possible," Mr. Peregrine allowed.

"You, perhaps?" Miss Booth asked, and grinned at him.

"No, no," Mr. Peregrine said. "I have no interest in ruining Mr. Laird, or in taking over a gaming establishment of this kind. All of my enterprises are on land and are a hundred percent legal."

"There are only two other possibilities," Miss de Lune said. "Either a member of the crew wants the *Lucky Duck* to fail or we're dealing with a real ghost."

"One thing is certain," Polly said, "if we catch the ghost, he'll be able to tell us something useful."

"He might be in here right now," Miss Booth said as she starred around at the nearly empty room.

Miss de Lune rubbed her arms with her hands. "Thank you Miss Booth. I now really and truly have the creeps."

Mr. Kepler rushed into the big room. "I understand you wanted to see me," he said as he crossed to True and Polly, and pulled up a chair.

"Don't sit down," True said. "I want you to show me around the museum again."

Mr. Kepler glanced around at the other guests. They watched him carefully.

"Certainly," Mr. Kepler said. "This way, please."

Mr. Kepler led them back along the main corridor. He unlocked the door to the museum and switched on the lights as he, True, and Polly entered. The big table still took up most of the room, and the playing cards were as Polly and the others had left them.

"No one has been in here to clean up I see," True said.

"I thought you might want to look for clues," Kepler said.

"Very considerate of you," True remarked. "Would it be possible for me to get another look at the display case where you keep the captain's weapons?"

"Of course," Mr. Kepler said. "You believe the murder weapon came from that case?"

"It's unlikely that it came from anywhere else," True said as he took the dagger from his pocket and held it out for Mr. Kepler's inspection.

"You can't buy a knife like that in housewares at a department store," Polly added.

"I suppose not." Mr. Kepler put out one hand as if to touch the dagger, then pulled it back quickly.

"What can you tell me about it?" True asked.

"I've been told it's a Turkish dagger, an eighteenth-century Ottoman jambiya. It has a real Damascus blade overlaid with gold using the koftgari method. The hilt is of walrus ivory. The green stuff covering the scabbard is supposed to be snake skin.

"It is beautiful," Polly said as she studied the dagger over True's shoulder, "in its own terrible way."

"You seem to know an awful lot about it," True said.

"I've done some research," Mr. Kepler admitted. "And I probably shouldn't tell you this," he continued ruefully, "but this dagger is one of my favorites among the captain's weapons."

"Such an admission won't do you much harm either," True said. "It is a beautiful piece. Let's have a look at the case."

Mr. Kepler led them across the room. True was surprised to see the cabinet doors were still closed, but the glass had been shattered and the shards were all over the floor. Behind the place where the doors closed together was a darker spot where the dagger had been displayed.

"Well, the murderer had to get to the dagger somehow," True said.

"Obviously, the murderer is someone who didn't have a key to the case," Mr. Kepler said.

"Who does have a key?" Polly asked.

"I do, of course," Mr. Kepler said. "And then there's

Miss Núñez and Mr. Laird."

"I want to make sure this dagger really came from here," True said. "Let's see if we can put it back." True attempted to slide the dagger behind the place where the doors met, but it was too long—it refused to fit behind the frame.

Mr. Kepler pulled the doors open and allowed True to try again. The dagger fit neatly into the empty spot.

"Very nice," True remarked. "Now all we have to do is find someone who doesn't have a key."

"That would be everybody on board except for the three I mentioned," Mr. Kepler said. "I suppose that includes Captain Robbins." He, True, and Polly had a polite chuckle over that.

"Tell me, Mr. Kepler," Polly said, "what is your feeling about ghosts? Do you believe Captain Robbins killed Mr. Cathcart?"

"I thought I made my opinion about real ghosts fairly clear when we were speaking with Zoltan. I am, shall we say, a skeptic, but I am willing to be convinced. At the moment I don't believe any more than you do that the Captain Robbins seen on this ship is a ghost. However, it is possible that a live person masquerading as Captain Robbins might had killed Mr. Cathcart."

"Thank you, Mr. Kepler," True said. "Very illuminating."

Mr. Kepler asked if there was anything else he could do for Mr. True or Miss St. Jough, and they assured him that they were all right as they were. "Oh, there is one thing," True said as Mr. Kepler was about to walk

out the door. "Could you ask that waiter—what's his name? The one with the big mustache.…"

"I think his name is Walter," Polly supplied.

"Yes, Walter. Could you ask him to come see me in my room? No hurry. I just have a few questions."

Mr. Kepler nodded and went on his way, leaving True and Polly to contemplate the smashed case. "I guess it couldn't have been Mr. Kepler," Polly said. "He would have no reason to smash the glass if he has a key."

"You may be right," True admitted. "Unless he wanted to mislead us. Let's go talk to Walter."

Polly squinted with concentration as True took her arm and escorted her out of the museum. With each thinking private thoughts, they walked through the big ship and came at last to the stateroom that had been assigned to True. True unlocked the door and allowed Polly to precede him. She opened a porthole to let in some air, then sat down on a chair by the dressing table and removed one slipper, allowing her easy access to a foot, which she rubbed vigorously. Meanwhile True paced.

There was a knock at the door, and True opened it expecting Walter Peevy, the waiter with the big mustache. But True made no welcoming noises, and instead backed into the room with his hands up.

CHAPTER EIGHT
TWO VISITORS

Forcing True into the room at the point of a small pistol was Clair de Lune.

"I know what you're thinking," Miss de Lune said.

"Oh?" True said with no more than polite curiosity.

"You're thinking that Brad killed Mr. Cathcart."

"Am I?"

"You know they didn't get along."

"From what I saw, Mr. Cathcart didn't get along with anybody. May I put my hands down? I'm starting to lose circulation in my fingers."

Miss de Lune actually seemed to think over True's request, but her pistol did not waver.

"I don't know what you expect to gain by threatening me," True said, "but I guarantee you won't be doing yourself or Brad any favors if you shoot me."

"Then tell me what I want to know."

"I will if I can."

"What evidence do you have against Brad?"

"Not very much," True admitted. "Just what you've already pointed out, that he and Mr. Cathcart didn't get along."

There was a knock at the door, and Miss de Lune didn't quite catch herself as she started to glance over her shoulder. This sudden lack of attention gave Polly the opportunity to throw her slipper at Miss de Lune, knocking the pistol from her hand. True immediately stepped forward and picked it up. "Very nice," he said, "a diamond-studded pearl-handled pistol. Twenty-two caliber, I'd say."

"Brad gave it to me," Miss de Lune said sounding miserable.

"For protection at Hollywood parties, no doubt," Polly said. "Very wise."

True opened the door, allowing Walter Peevy to enter. He seemed a little bewildered by the scene before him. "I can come back later if you're busy," he said.

"No, no. Miss de Lune was just leaving." He slipped the pistol into his pocket.

Miss de Lune looked as if she were about to protest, but decided against it. With some embarrassment, she left quickly without saying another word.

"Mr. Kepler said you wanted to see me," Peevy said.

"That's right," True said. "Have a seat. Take a load off."

"We're not supposed to sit with the guests."

"Don't worry about that. I'll square it with Mr. Laird this once."

Looking unhappy, Peevy lowered himself into a chair next to the door, but used only the front inch or so. He wasn't ready to use the whole chair in front of a guest no matter what the guest claimed he could

square.

"Comfortable?" True asked with only slight sarcasm.

"Yes, sir."

"I believe you and Miss Ogden discovered Mr. Cathcart's body. Isn't that correct?

"Yes, sir."

"Perhaps you noticed the murder weapon."

"It was a knife, sir."

"Not just a knife," True explained. "An eighteenth-century Turkish jambiya."

Peevy nodded.

"It came from a case in the ship's museum. Do you know anything about that?"

"I know the case is kept locked, sir. And that I don't have a key."

"Do you know who does have a key?"

"I can guess, sir. Mr. Laird. Maybe others. It's not really my business to know."

"Of course not," Polly said sympathetically.

"Where were you at the time the murder was probably committed?" True asked.

"Most of the time I was in the kitchen. There was not much to do with all the guests at the big ghost roundup."

True laughed at Peevy's description of the séance. "And the rest of the time?"

"I delivered a bottle of bourbon to Zoltan in his room."

"Was Zoltan there when you delivered it?"

"He was. It was almost eleven."

"That is something of an alibi for both of you," True suggested. He thought for a moment. "You didn't seem to like Mr. Cathcart very much yourself."

"That's right, sir. As you know, sir, I was not alone. As a matter of fact I—"

Peevy was interrupted by a shot from a pistol that True saw being pulled back through the porthole. As blood began to stain his shirt, Peevy sagged and slid onto the floor. While Polly saw what she could do for the wounded waiter, True ran to the porthole and looked out.

"How's he doing?" True asked as he turned to Polly and her patient.

"I'm afraid he's dead," Polly said, and stood up. "Did you see who did it?"

"Whoever fired the shot was long gone by the time I got to the porthole. No one was on deck. But the culprit was probably the same person who killed Mr. Cathcart."

"You think?" Polly asked, amazed.

"Sure. He thought Ol' Walter, here, was about to tell me who done it."

"Wasn't he?"

"I don't think so. If he knew who did the deed, and he was willing to volunteer the information, why would he wait so long to get around to telling me?"

"Then what was he going to tell you?"

"Your guess is as good as mine. We may never know." He studied the back of the chair Peevy had been sitting on and found a hole in it. Using his penknife, he

dug out the slug. "Looks like a thirty-eight."

"We'll search the ship," Polly proposed.

"It could take days to search a ship this size. And even if we find a pistol that will shoot a thirty-eight slug, we have no way to run a ballistics test and prove it was the pistol that shot him."

"And so?"

"And so, I'm going to call Otto and tell him we have a second candidate for his refrigerator."

CHAPTER NINE
THE GHOST SPEAKS

They called Mr. Laird, and he arrived with a couple of big crewmen who took Walter Peevy down to join Mr. Cathcart in the refrigerator.

"Two murders now," Mr. Laird said as he wiped the back of his neck with a handkerchief.

"I think the chances of there being any more are slim," True said, "but you never know."

"Have you any idea who is responsible?"

"I have some idea," True told him, "but so far the evidence is fairly circumstantial—the sort of thing a good lawyer could make mincemeat out of."

"Then what are you going to do?" Mr. Laird asked. He sounded as if he were at the end of a very short rope.

"Oh, what I must," True said casually.

"A habit he's gotten into," Polly confided.

When Mr. Laird and his men had gone with the body, True and Polly agreed that they both could use a drink. It had been a busy evening.

In no particular hurry they walked to Neptune's Hideaway. The lights were still on, but the big room

was empty, without even a musician or a waiter to enliven the place. True went behind the bar and mixed up a couple of gin and tonics. He and Polly sipped as they strolled to their rooms. The ship was very quiet except for the bass thrum of the engines, the far away lament of the fog horn, and another, very different, noise.

"What's that?" Polly asked.

"Rats in the walls?" True suggested.

"At least we know the ship isn't sinking," Polly replied.

They rounded a corner and nearly ran into Mr. Kepler.

"Hello there, old man," True said heartily. "I thought we were the last two abroad tonight."

"You almost were," Mr. Kepler said. "I was about to turn in when I heard a sort of rustling in the walls."

"Like rats?" Polly offered.

Mr. Kepler nodded. "You heard it too?"

"We did," True said. "You can escort us to our rooms," he went on. "Strength in numbers, and all that."

Mr. Kepler agreed and they ambled down the hall together, stopping now and then to listen.

"I was thinking of asking Zoltan to conduct another séance," True informed him.

"Whatever for?" Mr. Kepler asked.

"This time I want him to try contacting Mr. Cathcart. Perhaps he can tell us who murdered him."

"A waste of time, if you ask me."

"I think the noise is getting closer," Polly reported.

They continued down the hallway, walking carefully as if they feared landmines.

It seemed that the rustling was just around a bend in the corridor. Then something very near moaned. They stopped and prepared themselves as best they could. As True expected, Captain Robbins strode around the bend. He stood in the middle of the corridor swinging his saber and moaning. His heavy brocade outfit rustled, sounding like restless rats, as he moved.

Before True could stop him, Mr. Kepler pulled a pistol from his coat pocket and fired at the captain, who clutched his arm where a red blotch started to spread. Polly gave a little yelp of surprise. The captain ran back along the hall the way he had come. Guests, many of whom seemed to have rooms in this part of the ship, peeked around their doors to see what the commotion was.

True twisted the pistol from Mr. Kepler's hand and aimed it at him while noting it was a thirty-eight police special. Miss Booth, dressed in a wildly flowered bathrobe, and a rubbery-looking turban wrapped around her hair, was the first to hurry up to them. "What's the story?" she asked.

"We have our murderer," True said.

"What?" Mr. Kepler demanded. "That's ridiculous. Just because I took a shot at the ghost?"

"I'm afraid there's more to it than that," True said. By this time the other guests, in robes, dressing gowns, and pajamas, had gathered around yammering

questions at him. He handed the pistol to Miss Booth. "Don't let him get away," he ordered. "And somebody get Mr. Laird. He'll want to be in on this. I'll be back in a few minutes to explain. Get everyone into Neptune's Hideaway." Without waiting for a response, he ran after Captain Robbins. Polly was right behind him.

"I'll sit on him if I must," Miss Booth called enthusiastically.

True hurried around the corner and saw that a few yards beyond, drops of blood darkened the peach-colored carpeting. He and Polly followed the trail to a blank peach-colored wall—a dead end.

"Now what?" Polly asked.

"Now I do my famous Sherlock Holmes impression," True said as he got down on his hands and knees and carefully studied the line where the carpeting met the wall. "Look here," he went on. "This dust has been disturbed."

Polly looked closely. "And there," she said triumphantly, "is half a drop of blood."

"The other half must be behind the wall."

There was also a fan pattern where a door, or something like it, had swung open across the carpeting.

True stood a few steps back from the wall, confronting it as if it were an opponent. "If I were really Sherlock Holmes," he admitted, "I'd have a magnifying glass."

"Do you need one?" Polly asked.

"It can be a useful prop," True said as he took a step toward the wall. "Look here." He pointed at one of the rivets in a vertical line that held the wall panel in place.

"More blood," Polly noted.

"Yes."

True pushed the rivet and was delighted when something inside the wall clicked and the whole panel went in a little, then bounced out a few inches as if on a spring. True pulled the panel open, renewing the fan pattern in the carpet. Beyond was a narrow passageway lit by a bare low wattage bulb.

"Stay here," True said as he entered the passageway.

Polly ignored him. She pushed him ahead of her and pulled the panel closed using a handle she found on the inner side. True glared at her, but said nothing.

The walls of the passageway were painted a red so deep it was almost maroon. The naked bulbs revealed only enough to make the place seem more gloomy. True and Polly moved silently along the passageway following the trail of blood. Layers of dust lined the walls, but there was a clear path down the center of the passageway where the dust had been disturbed. Apparently the passageway had been had been used often, at least lately.

The passageway twisted and turned, and occasionally split, making a real maze. The only thing that kept them on track was the drops of blood, which became larger and more frequent.

Polly set her hand on True's shoulder, stopping him. She pointed down the passageway where a few yards away an open door allowed bright light to spill from the room beyond. Inside the room someone was moving around frantically.

"I wish I had a pistol," True whispered. To which Polly could only nod.

True and Polly crept forward silently; when they reached the doorway, True pushed Polly back and peeked around the jamb. The room seemed to be crowded with sailing paraphernalia: ropes, nets, clothing (some of which looked modern, and some of which looked as if it were from an earlier century), tools, and a large standing mirror—the same sort of stuff that was displayed in the ship's museum, but not nearly as well organized. The captain danced in front of the mirror changing clothes as rapidly as she could while favoring her injured arm. She had tied a wad of tissue around it, but blood was already soaking through.

"Is that you, Miss Núñez?" True asked.

The captain froze, then turned her head to look at him. She was halfway between characters; she still wore the beard and long hair, but she was wearing Miss Núñez's modern clothing. She slowly pulled the beard loose while staring at him speculatively. True was aware of Polly coming up behind him.

"I like you better without the beard," Polly remarked.

"So do I," Miss Núñez said. "It itches." She threw the beard and her long pirate coat onto a pile of tarpaulins, and pulled off the long black ringlets of her wig. The tricorn pirate hat went with it onto the tarp.

"How long have you known it was me?" Miss Núñez asked as she rubbed her face with cream.

"Since the séance. You were there at the door and

then you were gone."

"I might have had work to do."

"You might. I only suspected. I didn't know for sure until I saw you in between characters."

"What I want to know," Polly said, "is *why*?

"And *how*?" True added.

"*How* is simple enough," Miss Núñez said. She gently touched her injury and winced. "I was straightening Mr. Laird's office one day, going through a lot of junk left over from previous administrations, when I came across a stack of blueprints showing the ship— the *Hippocampus* as it was then—in great detail. The secret passages were there for anybody with the proper training to see."

"You have the proper training, Miss Núñez?" Polly asked.

"I do. It wasn't easy to get into the school, and many of my fellow students, all male, didn't approve, but I managed to get a degree in industrial engineering."

"Judging by your present employment," True said, "getting a job in your chosen field was something else again."

"As you can see," Miss Núñez agreed. "I was going to give the plans to Mr. Laird for the museum, and then I had a better idea."

"I think we're getting to *why* at last," Polly said.

"Did you find Captain Robbins' treasure?" True asked.

"As far as I can tell there is no treasure, just some rooms filled with the same kind of junk as you see all

around you here in this one."

"Then, to quote Miss St. Jough, '*why*'?"

"I didn't kill anybody, if that's what you mean."

"I didn't think you had. We have our suspect. It's Mr. Kepler."

Miss Núñez recoiled as if True had struck her. "Are you sure?"

"As sure as I can be without getting a confession. You can join the guests in Neptune's Hideaway if you want to hear my explanation."

"I'd like that," Miss Núñez admitted.

"She needs a doctor," Polly suggested.

"There's always one on board," Miss Núñez said. "I believe Dr. Birnberg is on duty."

"We'll send for him," Polly assured her. "Now, *why*?"

Miss Núñez smiled ruefully at her. "I wanted to buy the ship from Mr. Laird, run the place myself, but I did not want to pay the price he was sure to ask for it. So I thought if I could discourage clientele from showing up, I might be able to knock the price down a little. I wasn't sure at first that my idea would work. A ghost might attract customers rather than chase them away. But I got lucky. Everybody is lucky here on the *Lucky Duck*. What will you do with me, Mr. True?"

"Remembering that there is no law against dressing up," Polly reminded him.

"I'll take you to Mr. Laird," True said. "You tell him your story. You might be able to make a deal."

"In a moment," Miss Núñez said. "I have to complete my transformation." With her good arm, she

ran a brush through her real hair, and expertly applied lipstick. "Ready," she said.

CHAPTER TEN
LOOSE ENDS

True expected her to lead them back the way they had come, but instead she took them through a secret panel that put them just outside Neptune's Hideaway. All the guests were there as well as a few of the waiters and musicians who clumped together across the room watching the proceedings worriedly. Mr. Kepler was sitting on the edge of the stage. As promised, Miss Booth was sitting on his lap. Mr. Kepler wasn't comfortable, but Miss Booth ignored his pleas for her to get off him. Polly hurried over to Mr. Laird, who sat at a table in quiet discussion with Zoltan. She spoke to Mr. Laird briefly, nodded at Miss Núñez, and he hurried off.

True took the pistol from Miss Booth and she allowed Mr. Kepler to rise. He looked rumpled and unhappy as he ran one hand through his hair and glared at True. "You are in big trouble," he said.

"Perhaps," True admitted. He was about to start his explanation when Mr. Laird hurried in with a middle-aged man wearing a brown suit and big round glasses. Without a word the man in the brown suit opened his black bag and went to work on Miss Núñez.

"Well?" Mr. Kepler asked confidently.

"First there is the matter of the shattered glass case," True said.

"I had no need to shatter the case to get at the dagger," Mr. Kepler said. "As you may recall, I have a key."

"Indeed. And that turns out to be very important for a few reasons. First: though there was glass all over the floor, none of it was inside the case itself. Which means that somebody had to open it with a key before they knocked out the glass."

"Even so," Mr. Kepler said, "I am not the only person on the ship who had a key. Mr. Laird has one, as well as Miss Núñez. There may be others."

"There may be," True agreed pleasantly. "That is why my second point is also inconclusive: When I tried to return the dagger behind the closed doors, I failed. Even with the glass broken, unless the door is opened, the frame of the door blocks the way."

"That still proves nothing," Mr. Kepler said. "There are a lot of keys around."

"Quite right. But I think you'll find my third point is a lulu: When we went back to the case so I could return the dagger, you neglected to turn off the alarm before you opened the case. Only the murderer would assume the alarm had been disabled because he disabled it himself when he took the dagger to use on Mr. Cathcart."

With a sudden wild look in his eye, Mr. Kepler leaped to his feet and ran from the room. True fired at him and missed, allowing Mr. Kepler to escape. In

a moment True was after him, with Polly and most of the guests trailing behind like the tail of a comet. Mrs. Cathcart and Mr. Fields remained seated. They seemed only moderately interested—as if they were observing the performance of a play.

Heavy footsteps thundering, Mr. Kepler led them out onto the deck, where True took another few shots at him. Ducking behind companionways and metal supports, Mr. Kepler managed to avoid them all. He surprised the three water taxi pilots, slugged Manny, and quickly rummaged in his pockets until he found the green key that matched the hull of Manny's water taxi. He ran across the landing stage, leaped into the water taxi, and in seconds was booming toward Santa Monica, leaving a deep swish of wake.

"Give me your key," True demanded from Mo, who fumbled for a moment, and then produced it. True grabbed it and hustled across the landing stage after Mr. Kepler. He leaped into the blue water taxi, gunned the engine, and set out after the green water taxi.

The fog was gone and a bright moon shown on the water, touching the tops of waves with silver and making everything seem a little unreal.

True drove standing up, and cold salty spray stung his face. The taxis were equally matched, and though True didn't lose him, Kepler managed to maintain his lead.

True was surprised when the third taxi, the red one, angled toward the green taxi from one side carrying Polly and Miss Booth. Polly looked grim,

but Miss Booth, who was riding shotgun, was smiling and waving one arm as if she'd never had such fun. Apparently, the red taxi was supercharged in some way because it had no trouble catching up with Mr. Kepler. True frantically motioned for Polly to turn away, but she paid no attention and rammed Mr. Kepler's taxi hard from the side. Flinders of wood flew into the air as both boats seemed to explode on contact.

Someone on the *Lucky Duck* thought to turn on one of the big searchlights and shine it where the two boats had crashed together. The thick pencil of white light made rescuing the two woman easier.

Wishing his boat could go faster, True motored to the scene of the collision and pulled the two women from the water. They wrapped themselves in blankets they found under the seats while True throttled his engine down to a putter as he looked for Mr. Kepler among the wreckage. Despite the searchlight, and the fact that three pairs of eyes were peering into the water, Mr. Kepler seemed to be gone for good.

When the three returned to the *Lucky Duck*, Miss Núñez had a steaming pitcher of Irish coffee waiting for them. True sat near Polly and Miss Booth, who were still dripping a little. All three of them shivered despite the Irish. They sipped gratefully while Miss Núñez stood by with her arm in a fresh white sling. Mr. Laird sat nearby contemplating her as if she were full of possibilities.

"Have you and Mr. Laird had your little talk?" True asked Miss Núñez.

"We have," Miss Núñez said, "and I believe we are about to come to an understanding."

"If I let her buy half the business, she offers to stop haunting my ship," Mr. Laird said. "I'm still trying to decide whether that's a good deal."

"May I make a suggestion?" Miss de Lune inquired tentatively.

"Of course," Mr. Laird said and bowed a little without actually getting up.

"I've been thinking about what Mr. True said about the excitement in *The Mill on the Floss*."

"I hope you didn't take my remarks personally," True said.

"Of course not. But there is such a thing as taking one's self too seriously." She touched Brad Windsor's hand and smiled, pleasing him. "Instead of acting in a version of Miss Eliot's novel, perhaps I could star in a dramatization of the murder mystery we've all been through in the past few hours."

"I could write the scenario," Miss Booth cried with delight.

"Truth is," Mr. Peregrine said, "I was never very optimistic about a picture made from Miss Eliot's novel. But I would be delighted to invest a few bucks in *Murder on the Lucky Duck*, or whatever Miss Booth decides to call it."

Mrs. Cathcart spoke up suddenly. "I assume Miss de Lune will play the detective," she said.

Miss de Lune confirmed Mrs. Cathcart's guess.

"Very well," Mrs. Cathcart said. "Then I will also

invest."

Mr. Fields stared at her with surprise.

"I'm sure your husband would have approved," Polly said.

"I will invest anyway. It is not Miss de Lune's fault that my husband was an idiot."

"We could make a great picture right here on the *Lucky Duck*," Miss de Lune said. "If Mr. Laird agreed to take Miss Núñez in as a partner."

Mr. Laird looked at the floor between his feet and shrugged. Then he rose and went to Miss Núñez. He took her good hand and shook it. That seemed to settle the matter of Miss de Lune's movie.

"What now?" Mr. Laird asked True.

"The investigation is over," Miss Booth said. "That's for sure. It's obvious that Mr. Kepler was the murderer."

True appeared sad. "Correct," he said. "We can guess that he killed Walter Peevy because he thought Peevy was about to reveal him as Mr. Cathcart's murderer. What we may never know is why he murdered Mr. Cathcart in the first place."

After a long thoughtful silence, Mrs. Cathcart spoke up. "I know why," she said. "Or at least I can guess." Mr. Fields was having a bad night—Mrs. Cathcart continued to surprise him.

"You have our complete attention," True assured her.

Mrs. Cathcart sighed. "As you may have noticed, my husband was not a popular character, not even with me. What you probably didn't know was that Mr. Kepler was my brother."

True and Polly shared a glance. "Go on, Mrs. Cathcart," True urged. "You fascinate me strangely."

"My brother saw that he had the opportunity to do me a favor, to save me from the continuing unpleasantness of a loveless marriage."

"His action seemed a little extreme," Polly pointed out.

"Not from my point of view," Mrs. Cathcart snapped.

They all thought that over for a moment. "Any ideas on what Walter Peevy was about to tell me when Mr. Kepler shot him?" True asked.

"You mean he wasn't about to tell you that Kepler killed Cathcart?" Mr. Peregrine asked.

"I don't believe so. As I suggested to Polly at the scene of the crime, if Walter Peevy knew who did the deed, and he was willing to volunteer the information, I don't think he would have waited so long to tell me about it." True stared inquisitively at Mrs. Cathcart.

"I'm only guessing, of course," Mrs. Cathcart said, suddenly nervous.

"Go on," True said. "We're all friends here."

"I think he was going to talk about his own connection with my husband," Mrs. Cathcart said. "Their relationship went back a few years. Peevy had been a steward at the Bangor Professional Club until he had a public disagreement with Mr. Cathcart and he had Peevy fired."

"That's all?" Polly asked.

"That might be enough for some people," Mrs. Cathcart replied. "After all, Peevy only spilled a drink

on my husband—he didn't kill him."

"If we are no longer suspects," Mr. Fields said, "I for one would like to get off this ship of fools."

"I understand," True said. "You can come with me on the one remaining taxi when I take our two victims back to Santa Monica. What about you, Mrs. Cathcart?"

Before Mrs. Cathcart could speak up, Mr. Laird offered the hospitality of the ship to her and to anyone else who wanted to stay for another few days. "If my partner agrees," he said, and nodded at Miss Núñez.

"Of course," she said, and smiled brilliantly.

"I'll stay," Mrs. Cathcart said. "I have nothing in particular to go home to."

Clair de Lune, Brad Windsor, and Miss Booth also decided to take advantage of Mr. Laird's offer; they wanted to scout locations and otherwise discuss *Murder on the Lucky Duck*.

"I think I'll stay too," Polly said. "That way you're more likely to come back, and we can have a real vacation. Please give my regards to Lieutenant Ochoa."

"Sneaky," True said.

ABOUT THE AUTHOR

MEL GILDEN is the author of many children's books, some of which received rave reviews in such places as *School Library Journal* and *Booklist*. His multi-part stories for children appeared frequently in the *Los Angeles Times*. His popular novels and short stories for grown-ups have also received good reviews in the *Washington Post* and other publications. (See new publications under his name at the Kindle Store of Amazon.com, at iTunes, and his website, www.melgilden.com.)

Licensed properties include adaptations of feature films, and of TV shows such as the *Jungle Book*, *Beverly Hills 90210*, and *NASCAR Racers*. He has also written books based on video games, and has penned original stories based in the *Star Trek* universe. His short stories have appeared in many original and reprint anthologies.

He has written cartoons for TV, has developed new shows, and was assistant story editor for the DIC television production of *The Real Ghostbusters*. He consulted at Disney and Universal, helping develop theme park attractions. Gilden also spent five years as

co-host of the science-fiction interview show, *Hour-25*, on KPFK radio in Los Angeles.

Gilden lectures to school and library groups, and has been known to teach fiction writing. He lives in Los Angeles, California, where the debris meets the sea, and still hopes to be an astronaut when he grows up.